THE 88 BUS

AND OTHER SHORT STORIES

THE 88 BUS

AND OTHER SHORT STORIES

IVOR RAWLINSON

Matador
Unit E2 Airfield Business Park,
Harrison Road, Market Harborough,
Leicestershire. LE16 7UL
Tel: 0116 2792299
Email: books@troubador.co.uk
Web: www.troubador.co.uk/matador
Twitter: @matadorbooks

ISBN 978 1803136 936

British Library Cataloguing in Publication Data.
A catalogue record for this book is available from the British Library.

Printed and bound in Great Britain by 4edge Limited
Typeset in 11pt Aldine401 BT by Troubador Publishing Ltd, Leicester, UK

Matador is an imprint of Troubador Publishing Ltd

For Catherine

CONTENTS

The 88 Bus   1

Cardiology Clinic   6

The Old World   11

Are We Too Early?   16

The Postman   21

Neighbourhood Watch   26

The Bodyguard   31

The Bench   36

The Queen's Birthday Party   41

Tour de France   46

The Revolution   51

The Barber   56

The Deal   61

Tree Power   66

Beaver Lake   71

Always Believe   76

The Passenger Locator Form   81

Tango   86

The Last Laugh   91

The Cabin   96

THE 88 BUS

As a woman, I'm very careful about where I sit on the bus. Back row on the top deck is asking for trouble. I suppose downstairs near the doors or the driver are safe places, but you don't get the view. And the views from the number 88 are worth having. So, I chose the front seat over the driver on the top deck last week, when coming back to Clapham from Charing Cross Road. It was late morning on a Wednesday and I had been to a bookshop there to collect a first edition of *Dunbar's Complete Handbook of Etiquette* for my husband's birthday. That's the great thing about being a collector; bookshops ring you when they've got something they know you will like. Makes birthdays easy.

The bus was not very full when I got on at Trafalgar Square and I thought I would remain undisturbed. No such luck. Halfway down Whitehall, about six more passengers boarded. The last of them was a priest, around forty-five years old, I would say, all dressed in black. I should have continued looking out of the window at Banqueting House and the Ministry of Defence, but I made the great mistake of looking at his face – and half-smiling. Needless to say, he sat beside me, smoothing his black raincoat under his backside and settling himself comfortably.

It was only then that I noticed two things. His breath smelt ever so slightly of beer, and he had a broad blue ribbon round his neck, which held in place a small wooden tray holding some pamphlets and a collection tin.

"Sorry," he said, as the wooden tray grazed my knee.

"Quite alright," I said and turned to look out of the window again. A straggle of bored-looking protesters were behind a dozen wire barriers between the Ministry of Defence and – is it the Ministry of Health? They were shouting without much conviction towards Downing Street on the other side of the road.

"Anti-immigration layabouts," said the priest, nodding to where I was looking. Not quite the language I expected from a man of the cloth. Then, I saw a badly drawn placard – 'KEEP THEM IN CALAIS'. A single policewoman in a high-vis jacket gazed at us in the bus. She was as bored as the pathetic protestors.

As the electric bus moved smoothly towards Parliament Square, I tried to read the title of one of the pamphlets in the tray beside my legs. I assumed it was something religious, but could only make out 'Bling', 'A curse' and 'My Story'.

Unfortunately, the priest caught me looking.

"Are you a Catholic?" he said, accompanied by a little waft of beer.

"As it happens, I am," I replied.

"Well, there's a ting," he said. "So am I." He smiled and I could see he had bad teeth. Still, I smiled weakly back.

I felt much more at ease all of a sudden. I also recognised an Irish accent, which, for some unknown reason, I have always found a comfort. *How many Catholic priests in England are Irish?* I wondered.

"Are you going far?" he said, cheekily.

"Clapham," I replied, keeping my voice down, hoping he wouldn't hear. By now, the bus was near the end of Marsham Street. In the sunlight, the Home Office building looked less forbidding than usual.

"So am I. St Mary's actually." My heart sank. Not least because here was a holy father who smelt of drink. *But it takes all sorts to make a world*, I said to myself. *Nobody's perfect.*

"I've been collecting all morning," he said.

"Oh really. What for?"

"To save addicted gamblers. Jesus knew all about the evils of gambling, you know. Like so much of what Jesus said, you have to read between the lines. *'And every one who has left houses or brothers or sisters or father or mother or children or lands, for my name's sake, will receive a hundred-fold and inherit eternal life. But many that are first will be last, and the last first.'* – Matthew 19."

He was warming to his theme. We were at the Tate Gallery and I wondered whether to ring the bell and get off the bus. But I didn't of course. I studied instead the yellow, red and grey building next door to Tate Britain – the Chelsea College of Arts – looking for all the world like an Indian viceregal palace.

"You cannot imagine how many gambling addicts there are. They're often from broken homes. And from ethnic minorities. I am known as someone who can help. They come to confession. It's terrible what I've seen." He lowered his voice slightly. The two men in suits in the other front seats were clearly trying to listen. "So many young people, both sexes, simply cannot control their urge to gamble, even when they know the odds are against them."

We were crossing the river now. The highlight of the journey. I turned my head at right angles to admire the view. 'Earth has not anything to show more fair' wrote Wordsworth two hundred years ago on Westminster Bridge. I was desperately trying to think of anything but this, no doubt, worthy priest beside me.

He started again. "It's a form of escapism but the trouble is, it actually destroys relationships. Addicts lose interest in the rest of life. They live for the adrenalin rush they get going into a betting shop."

"Really?" I said. "And can they be helped?"

"Oh yes. With counselling. But it's expensive. That's what I'm collecting for." He touched the tin in his tray and as he did so, I noticed his dirty fingernails.

"It's an insidious human vice. They feel they cannot stop. So they often gamble in secret." He halted for a moment to see what effect he had had. Then, he made his last bid for my sympathy. "The suicide rate is appalling, you know, truly shocking."

The bus, by now, was in Clapham High Street. I could just see, out of the corner of my eye, one of the men in suits slowly shaking his head from side to side. I thought he was thinking, 'How awful'. It only occurs to me now that he was trying to signal something else to me.

"Next stop's my church," the priest said. He looked down again at his collection tin.

"Mine's the one after," I said.

I quietly reached for my purse, took out a ten-pound note and stuffed it into the tin.

"A true Christian," he said as he removed the ten pounds from the tin and put it into his pocket. He moved down the stairs and off the bus.

The bus was obviously ahead of schedule because the driver waited two minutes at the bus stop. From the window, I saw the priest take off his dog collar and stuff it into his raincoat pocket. He took off the tray, put it into a shopping bag and ran triumphantly into the betting shop.

CARDIOLOGY CLINIC

At the bottom of the electronic noticeboard in the cardiology clinic waiting area, a message flashed up preceded by three stars: '*Prof. Walker's clinic is running approximately one hour late. Please accept the hospital's apologies.*' This was greeted by crossings of legs and scarcely audible sighs of resignation or frustration from the dozen or so patients.

Two men in the middle of the front row, who previously had studiously avoided looking at each other, now did so. They were separated by a small, low table on which were some dog-eared copies of the hospital magazine and two dirty plastic cups. Both men were in their late sixties and well dressed. The one with neatly parted grey hair (we'll call him 'John') half-turned to the balding one, who was reading *The Economist* (we'll call him 'Simon').

"Probably had to do a quick heart transplant during the lunch hour," he joked in a low voice to his neighbour. "That's what's delayed him."

Simon smiled. "Yes. Afternoon appointments here are always late. What was your appointment time?"

"Three-fifty. And yours?"

"Three-thirty."

"Just twenty minutes per patient. It's not long, is it?"

The ice had been broken. But it was still thin and custom demanded both should skate carefully. It was already clear to both from dress, accent and other clues (leather shoes, signet ring) that they could have a conversation – indeed, that they wanted one. Complaining or moaning could be a common bond, a starting point.

"You'd think that a teaching hospital like this would have a better car park, wouldn't you?" asked Simon.

"Apparently, it's always been a problem. I came by tube actually."

"Ah. So not too far."

"Clapham." *That was quite precise enough at this stage*, thought John.

Right opposite our two gentlemen, a West Indian lady wearing a blue Jackie Kennedy hat burst out of the consulting room, saying, "Bye, bye doctor." She stood still, confused, trying to get her bearings while a white coat quickly closed the door behind her and started dictating. A dozen faces stared at the noticeboard to see which name would come up next. Five minutes later, '*Adam Kucharski*' illuminated the screen, and a man and a woman responded at once and knocked on the consulting room door.

"I'm the other side of the river – Kensington," said Simon.

"Some lovely houses in Kensington," said John.

"I'm in a flat, actually," said Simon. "I never married. A beautiful girl broke my heart when I was twenty-two. Silly really, but I never found another like her."

"We've been nearly forty years in Clapham. Bought it for nothing and renovated it ourselves. Lucky I married a painter, decorator and electrician!"

Simon thought John's voice was vaguely familiar. "Were you…" – but he couldn't ask directly what work he did. It wouldn't be right. An invasion of privacy. So he changed the subject temporarily.

Simon looked longingly at a younger patient who had shown remarkable initiative by finding a cup of tea elsewhere in the building.

"Shall I ask where he got it and buy teas for us both?" said Simon. Drinking tea together would help surmount any inhibitions and any awkwardness in a conversation that wasn't getting very far.

"Risky," said John. "As soon as you're gone, your name will come up, you'll be marked as a 'no show' and you're back to your GP."

"You're right. One day without tea won't kill us, will it? Hospital tea's probably toxic anyway," said Simon.

John warmed to Simon. He had a sense of humour. Hospitals were not exactly relaxing places and the long delay was creating a bad atmosphere. A good talk with a fellow heart-sufferer would lift spirits and be an afternoon bonus.

"In the Civil Service, in the old days, about ten of us shared an enormous enamel teapot, which was strategically placed in the juniors' room. The head of department came at four every day and it was the perfect moment to find out what was going on with our ministers and so on," said John.

"I was in the Civil Service, too. Home Office. Emergency Planning Directorate."

"Extraordinary. I started off at Environment – flood defences. I was in the 1978 intake. We must have met," said John.

"It seems such a long time ago," said Simon. "Did you stay at Environment?"

So far, disclosure had been mutual. But now the first one to reveal his final job risked embarrassing the other in case the other hadn't done as well.

Modesty forbade John from admitting straightaway that he had risen to the very top, with a knighthood. He simply said, "I was lucky at the end. Right place at right time and a prime minister who knew me from old. We were at Oxford together – '74-'76. Christ Church."

"I thought the face was familiar. I was there, too. Same time. First year that girls were admitted to the college."

"Where did you end up?" asked John.

"Bit of a sideshow. Cabinet Office. Looking after Cobra and all that."

Both men were silent for a while as they digested all this. They knew each other's names, but there was something holding each of them back. The forty-four years flipped back like pages in an old photo album in both their minds.

"Didn't we act together? I mean, weren't you in *Pygmalion*?" asked John.

"Of course. You were Prof Higgins. I was backstage. And Eliza Doolittle was played by Jill Morpeth. Simon paused for a second. "She had exquisite green eyes framed by a fringe." He sighed. "Her hair smelt of green apples, I remember. A smile like no other. So gentle – and super intelligent. Do you remember, she used to tilt her head slightly when asking a question. We were madly in love for two years, then I went to London and she stayed on at Oxford and she fell silent. I was in despair. I don't know what happened."

John coughed and looked at his well-polished shoes. "I married her. Jill's my wife."

At that moment, Simon's name appeared on the noticeboard. As he stood up to go for his consultation, he turned back.

"You bastard," he said.

THE OLD WORLD

It was nine-fifteen exactly on a perfect mid-May morning as Herr Müller wheeled his bicycle the last few metres and leant it up against a post with the number '73' on it. The sun had already burnt off most of the dew from the rows of vegetables and fruit bushes. The dew still outlined a spider's web built between the door of his tool-shed and the spout of his aluminium watering can. Plants, grass and especially weeds were bursting with early summer life. Two large slugs had taken up positions at either end of his lettuces, just waiting for the moment to attack. Herr Müller smiled. The slugs were out of luck because he would be picking the biggest lettuce that very morning for his usual weekend salad.

Herr Müller was looking for some sign that would tell him that his allotment was too much for him now that he had turned eighty. Would the sign be backache after sowing his lines of runner beans? Would it be the failure of his asparagus? His asparagus had won a prize thirty years ago. The faded black and white newspaper photograph of him holding the vegetable was in a frame between his two kitchen cupboards back at the apartment.

What he feared most was that the Committee would pay an official visit to his allotment, which was admittedly close to the entrance gate, and strip him of his permit because of the weeds. That would be humiliating after thirty-five years. But each year since Christa's death, Herr Müller had found it increasingly difficult to keep his allotment tidy and weed-free. This spring had been the worst. Tidiness, Herr Müller believed, was really important. The weeds preyed on his mind. He had nightmares about them. He dreamt convolvulus had strangled his raspberry canes; giant dandelions had stopped his carrots growing; and brambles were throwing out shoots onto his neighbours' vegetables faster than he could pull them out.

Gardening for Herr Müller was a question of discipline. It was a question of man versus nature – a matter of control. So, for nature to gain the upper hand on his vegetable patch was a disaster. Another example of the chaos of which he was so fearful in his little world.

Herr Müller went to his allotment twice a week, on Tuesdays and Fridays. His routine was invariable. It was a fifteen-minute bicycle ride from Bockenheim to the allotments. He left his flat at 9am and he returned at noon on the dot. Today was a Friday. In the two and a half hours available, he had intended to turn over the soil at the far end of his patch and add in some compost. But it wasn't to be. His fork snapped three quarters of the way down as he pulled up the heavy earth. He knew the fork would break one day but he had been horrified by the price of a new one in the hardware store in Leipziger Strasse. Money had become very tight recently. His rent had been increased by five per cent; he had had to replace his gas-heater in the kitchen, which the plumber said was unsafe; and he had had to buy hearing aids that were unbelievably expensive (800 euros, minimum). For fully twenty minutes, Herr Müller sat in the old wooden kitchen chair beside his tool-shed just looking at the green explosion all around him, watching the blackbirds enjoying their worms – and thinking.

Despite the money problem, he realised full well how lucky he was. He had six good friends, all men and mostly widowers like himself. Four of them now had serious health problems – Alzheimer's, painful hip, dodgy heart and macular degeneration, to be exact. But he was as fit as a fiddle apart from his hearing. Actually, he counted his deafness as a blessing in a way. He could scarcely hear the barking dogs in the flats above and below his. Nor the racket from the bakery opposite from four in the morning.

And he had his interests – his allotment, the history of printing (typesetting had been his trade) and cooking. He had done the cooking even when Christa was alive. He reckoned he watched seven hours of cookery a week on television!

Two and a half hours at the allotment – no more, no less each time – passed quickly. Just before leaving, he picked up the two slugs and dropped them in his water butt. It had occurred to him to throw them onto his Turkish neighbour's allotment. But that would be un-German and petty-minded. So he didn't. By the time he had sliced off the biggest lettuce with his penknife to put in his bike basket, it was 11.45am. By midday, he was home. Having parked his faithful bicycle in the first rack on the left-hand side – always the same rack – he locked it, pocketed the key in his top shirt pocket with its key ring shaped like a heart (a gift from Christa long ago) and pulled down the top of the communal dustbin. *Why couldn't the dustmen close the lid?* He'd complained about it to the waste management office and had even had an unpleasant exchange of words with the dustmen themselves, who swore at him in Turkish or so he guessed. *It was such a simple gesture to close a dustbin*, Herr Müller thought. Symbolic of how standards had slipped. So disrespectful. Anyway, another key opened the back door to the little apartment block. He then took the lift to the third floor.

The apartment was modest – well, let's be truthful, it was small. Hall, kitchen, bathroom, living room and bedroom. There was a faint smell of sauerkraut – or was it furniture polish? Or both. He took off his shoes, placing them on the rectangular mat exactly beside the brown leather brogue shoes he would be wearing in the afternoon. He showered and changed into a blue cotton shirt, grey trousers – which he kept in his trouser press – and his collarless light green summer jacket. He used to wear a splash of *eau de cologne* after showering but he could no longer afford it. Anyway, he kept telling himself, it was unnecessary consumption. We needed to cut down on things like that. He had enough to live on after all. His state pension plus the small pension from Axel Springer publishing just about saw him through the month as long as there were no bad surprises – like having to buy a new garden fork.

Part of Herr Müller's recipe for a happy life – which his was – was order. When there was a routine, you knew where you were. Order was the sister of efficiency. Disorder meant chaos and Herr Müller had seen enough of that in his lifetime, thank you very much.

So, he had laid the table for lunch straight after breakfast. Friday lunch in summer was always raw celery with a line of salt down the middle of each stick, potato salad with chopped chives in the mayonnaise, and three slices of finely minced *Rindswürst,* sausage made from pure beef, a Frankfurt speciality. Fruit was a problem in May unless you wanted to eat stuff from the other side of the world with a huge carbon footprint. So, he usually had a couple of his own bottled plums. Or a tomato.

After he had done the washing up, there was one hour for reading and a nap. Because at three-thirty on Tuesdays and Fridays, he would walk to the end of the street, buy a newspaper, and take it into Ilse's café for tea and a piece of strudel. Regular as clockwork.

Ilse's café was next to the Post Office. As he approached it, one of those blue armoured security vans drove off. Quite slowly.

Outside the Post Office, at the edge of the pavement, he noticed a thick pile of twenty-euro banknotes – there must have been a hundred of them – in a paper wrapper. Nobody was looking so, with the toe of his brown shoe, he tapped the banknotes into the roadside drain and went for his afternoon tea.

ARE WE TOO EARLY?

"**M**ummy, there's a lady at the door and a man behind her. They've got a present for us, I think."

My four-and-a-half-year-old, Felicity, had just learnt how to open the front door. I had let her because I thought my husband, Richard, had left his keys behind when he rushed off to work this morning. It's a relatively safe part of Paris here. The embassy has rented this flat for at least six years. Our predecessor was doing the same job as Richard. Basically trying to discover how the French socialist government was being so successful with the economy and to see whether we could learn anything. Richard said the job was horse-trading, but I thought it sounded more like horse-stealing. There was no doubting the rivalry between our governments. And jealousy, in a way.

We had found that senior French officials and politicians really opened up over a meal at home. We had a good dining room and took a lot of trouble with our dinners. I think it helped that I am French. We were expected to entertain important contacts and were given an allowance for it. Not always easy if one has a young child at home like we do and no home help. I work full time, as I did before we married here.

I'm a picture restorer. On the day in question, everything went wrong. We'd just collected a Monet that the Louvre wanted restoring before its Impressionist show next year. It was heavy and needed three men to handle it because of its massive frame. There was no trouble on the short journey to our studio. But none of us checked my easel. The weight was too much and there was a splitting noise when it crashed onto the floor. The frame was damaged.

Then, when I picked up Felicity from school, her teacher was waiting for me. Apparently, Felicity had announced at the beginning of the school day, in a loud voice, that she was English and would not speak French any more. Indeed, despite the teacher's best efforts, Felicity only spoke English for the rest of the day. I smiled, but the teacher said it was no joke. "Imagine," she said, "in a cosmopolitan school like this, if everyone spoke in different languages. It would be chaos. Would you speak to your daughter so this does not happen again."

By the time I arrived home, I was feeling pretty low, to put it mildly. The flat was in a mess, which didn't help. There were toys everywhere and Richard had left the milk beside the fridge instead of in it. Had I not been pregnant, I would have had a glass of white wine. But I started unloading the dishwasher, then opening the post, then sitting down to read the letter from my mother.

I decided not to talk to Felicity about what had happened at school until I'd talked to Richard about it. She was finishing her meal of carrots, peas and fishcakes. She had insisted on squeezing tomato ketchup onto her plate all by herself. Most of it had squirted onto her chest and was running down to her waist when the doorbell rang. She ran to the door and opened it.

"Oh. Are we too early?"

I didn't recognise the voice. I had never seen the couple before. They were beautifully dressed. She wore a pleated beige skirt and expensive shoes. I stood motionless for a few seconds. The man, who was wearing a knitted blue tie that wasn't straight, stared at me.

"Hervé de Solignac," he said, rocking forward onto the balls of his feet. "And Madeleine, my wife."

Richard and I had agreed we'd have a dinner for three of his key contacts the following week. He was particularly excited because the President's economic advisor had agreed to come. He was said to be a rising star and tipped to be a minister. He only slept four hours a night, which Richard found incredible. I'd forgotten the name. I had to make a decision quickly.

"Of course. Come in," I said. I wished Richard was here; he was playing tennis.

"I'm sorry about the toys and things. Let me take your coat, Madeleine."

"This is for you," she said, handing me an expensive-looking triangular box with the name of a famous chocolate maker on a gold label. It was only then that I looked at her eyes, as one does when saying thank you. Her eye shadow was smudged and there was something funny about the eyes themselves.

"You have a lovely view of the park," the husband said,

as he zigzagged through a dolly's tea party on the living room floor.

While they were at the window, I picked up the newspapers and books from the top of the sofa and hid them under it.

Felicity said, "Mummy, why are you hiding things under—" until I put a finger to my lips.

When Hervé turned to look at Felicity, I noticed he had a bead of sweat running down his face. He asked where Richard was and I said he'd be coming shortly. He saw the ketchup on Felicity's dress and started to laugh in a high-pitched way. He seemed agitated. Felicity was scared of them both and hung on to my leg.

My mind was racing. There was no way I had food for the four of us unless I did something miraculous with pasta. I had four pork sausages, the remains of Felicity's supper and a baguette. In the freezer were ice lollies and a plastic bag on which I'd written "curry for one". Richard had said he would bring something home from the market for our supper that night.

"I'm sure you'd like a drink," I said, desperately trying to keep calm. Some of Felicity's ketchup had transferred itself to my skirt. When I brought in the whisky they had asked for, I said I would just see how things were in the kitchen. Hervé then asked if he could use the bathroom. As I led the way, Madeleine said, "Oh, do let me see the rest of the flat as well." She was studying the pictures on the wall by the bathroom when I said I'd be a couple of minutes in the kitchen and then I had to put Felicity to bed.

"They are very expensive chocolates. You can have one if you undress and clean your teeth by yourself and if you

19

put the box back where you found it." Never had Felicity gone to bed so easily.

At that moment, Richard came home, still in his tennis gear. There was no one in the kitchen or living room so he went to our bedroom, dropped his racquet on the bed and went straight to the bathroom. He looked at the couple there in utter amazement, then shouted, "What the hell!" and slammed the door. He met me in Felicity's room looking like he'd seen a ghost.

"I'm terribly sorry," I said. "Hervé de Solignac and his wife. Isn't he the one you said was very close to the President? Meant to be coming here next week? I thought I had to let them in."

"Yes. Correct on all points. That's the man. Never met Madame."

"I'm so, so sorry. I shouldn't have let them in. And I haven't got anything except sausages to give them."

"No need to be sorry. Do you know what they were doing? Snorting cocaine. Like pigs. In our bathroom, for God's sake. Useful to know. Let's get changed."

THE POSTMAN

Tony Edwards, the postman, knew the streets of
Ryde on the Isle of Wight off by heart. He reckoned
that even blindfolded, he could not only tell which
street he was in, but what end of the street. Part of it was
the feel of the paving stones through his trainers. Part of it
was the individual noise of each street. The streets by the
Esplanade had wave-breaking or flag-snapping noises. Or
the cries of children running to the sands. The streets at
the back of the town had quite different noises – girls at the
convent school, the sizzling from the fish and chip shop,
the barmaid dragging benches and tables together outside
the pub. Even the birds made different noises there. They
were songbirds, not seabirds.

Poor, run-down streets where the houses were close
together, like Nelson Street behind the Esplanade, had
echoes. The posher streets, with detached houses and
front gardens, had bad acoustics. His hearing was highly
developed ever since the music teacher at school had taken
him under his wing. He had been born with a remarkable
voice, but he had had a crippling stutter since he was five.

Tony had lived in Ryde all his life. He remembered only a few events from his very troubled earliest years when he seemed to be constantly moving from one room to another near the station at St John's. He never saw or knew his father. But he had fond memories of his mother. He remembered her bed – its softness, its warmth. She would hide underneath the blanket and make Tony laugh till he cried playing peek-a-boo. He remembered her telling the story of *Jack and the Beanstalk*, which usually ended with tummy-tickling. She relied on making a little money in summer by washing up in the cafés on the Esplanade. In winter, they were shut. And as more people chose to go to Rhodes rather than Ryde in the summer, the bucket-and-spade tourist trade died. It was the same in hundreds of English seaside towns. Truth to tell, they had been struggling for years. The local councils tried their best to tempt visitors back. They boasted about their sunshine records. They capitalised on the craze for dinosaurs. A Harry Potter castle replaced the slot-machine arcade. It was an ominous sign that a new tapas bar had to close because of aggressive seagulls. They stole the food before clients could eat it. Behind the painted facades, there was some of the worst poverty in Britain.

Tony and his mother were desperately poor. His only soft toy was a grey woollen rabbit. 'Bunny' was the first word he said, so that became Tony's nickname. All his clothes for primary school were second- or third-hand. Tony never starved, but his mother nearly did. In summer, she stole food from the cafés where she worked. In winter, they ate stale bread given to Tony's mum by the corner shop. The fruit they ate in summer was 'picked up' from the gardens of the big houses on East Hill – apples, the occasional fig, greengages and once, just once, a whole bag of strawberries.

He remembered his mother saying the Lord's Prayer, each of his hands in her hands. "Thy Kingdom come, Thy will be done, on Earth as it is in Heaven." After each three words or so, Mummy would look into his eyes. When she said, "Give us this day our daily bread," she would cry. She said, "I'm not crying really, darling." But she let go of his hands to wipe away her tears, so he knew.

His special memory was of his mother singing lullabies and hymns. Especially hymns, because she sang in the Catholic church choir at one time. There was usually cake and biscuits to be pocketed for Tony after church.

Then she was gone. The one person who loved him unconditionally, was gone. He was told ten years afterwards, by his music teacher, that she had multiple sclerosis and had been taken to a hospital in Portsmouth. The doctors said she was not fit to look after a child. She would be removed to Wales where she said her own mother came from. She disappeared from Tony's life until he was in his thirties when he had become a postman. One day, he noticed the name 'Edwards' on an envelope he had to deliver to a run-down fisherman's cottage in Nelson Street. But it was a common surname and he thought no more of it.

Tony spent the rest of his childhood in care. At the first home he was at, he cried for weeks on end. No one could replace his mother. Each time the doorbell rang, he looked expectantly in case there were two open arms and a big smile and she would say, "Darling Tony" and he would say, "Mummy" and she would not let go. But it never happened.

He stopped smiling aged five and a half. He went into a shell for six years. As he turned twelve and started at secondary school, the teachers wrote to the council that he was damaged; they said he was shy, anxious and bitter. He trusted no one. He stuttered very badly. He said the world was against him. The music teacher, Mr Atkins, was the only one Tony liked and could respect. He was the father he had never known. But Mr Atkins knew that he had a genuine singer on his hands, a very rare talent. He had been born with a pitch-perfect voice. Mr Atkins had read that singing was a therapy for stuttering. That proved to be only half-right. Mr Atkins taught Tony how to read music and about breath control, projection and tone. Best of all, Mr Atkins gradually made Tony sing with others. He got over his shyness.

So adolescent Tony found the support he needed in music. There were awful setbacks. He ran away from home aged fourteen, stole cash from a newsagent and was found, drunk and tearful, by the police on the other side of the Isle of Wight. Mr Atkins persuaded the magistrate that this was an aberration. Potential foster parents didn't want to take on someone with all of Tony's problems.

When he left school at sixteen with O-levels in Music and English, it was Mr Atkins who persuaded Tony to become a postman. Tony loved it. He liked the early morning starts. He liked the fact that regular customers were so friendly and said, "Good morning" and "Hello". He didn't mind collecting signatures for recorded deliveries, unless there were dogs. He had a system for shutting dogs up – he bared his teeth at them in a huge grin like Wallace in *Wallace & Gromit*. The dogs were puzzled and turned away.

Of course, there was a dreadful sadness in the background, like his heart had been broken and would never be repaired.

On the day of my story – a bright, sunny day in mid-March with no wind – Tony had been a postman in Ryde for twelve years. He was proud of what he had achieved. From seriously disturbed orphan with a stutter and a grudge, he had become a responsible young man, earning a wage.

Towards eleven in the morning, he found himself in the middle of Nelson Street, the one with run-down cottages but a great acoustic. It was deserted. Some daffodils were struggling on a scrap of earth underneath a chipped blue and white statuette of the Virgin Mary.

He carefully placed his postbag at his feet in the middle of the narrow street. With his hands clasped in front of him, he sang Schubert's 'Ave Maria', first softly, then in a swelling tenor until the windows rattled.

After two minutes, a middle-aged woman's face peeped round a rickety door to his left. Tears glistened in the sunlight as they ran down her cheeks.

"Bunny?" she whispered.

NEIGHBOURHOOD
WATCH

F oxwood Road is one of dozens of residential roads at right angles to Clapham Common. It would be ungentlemanly to reveal precisely which side of the triangular common it lies. In any case, the roads look very similar to the casual observer. They have the same history. Built by later Victorian speculators (sorry, developers) on the land behind the old mansions, the roads spread out like the light from an exploding star. They were built at pace to a pattern. There is a military symmetry to them. Cheek by jowl, fifty terraced houses line Foxwood Road on one side and fifty on the other. Looking from the Common end of the street, the houses look like a regiment standing to attention. The bay windows jut their chins out, the upper bay windows wear pointed slate helmets and the chimney pots above them stand guard till the sun goes down at the end of the street over Balham.

The coming of the train, the tram and, later, the underground meant office workers could live here and be in central London in less than an hour. The developers were catering for a burgeoning new class – the commuter. He was the family man who wanted his own place, privacy and comfort. He sought respectability above all else. His house had to be a cut above the flat-fronted, featureless houses for the lower class of office worker. But eccentricity was out of the question. Any individuality had to be minimal and was restricted to glazing on the front door or a non-standard front gate. There were no pubs and the roads were on the narrow side. A question of self-restraint.

For seventy years and through two world wars, not much changed in Foxwood Road save for the motor car – the key to family freedom. The road was decent, quiet and sober. Coal was delivered by coal merchants, poured from sacks down coal holes in the front path. It was burnt in the fireplaces built in each room. The milkman, the butcher, the baker and the fishmonger all delivered their goods, for there was always a maid or housewife at home. Front steps were scrubbed. A question of standards.

By the 1970s, Clapham had become a destination for a different sort of commuter – the young professionals. They worked in the City rather than the shops of the West End. They worked to a different rhythm. Their ethic was 'time is money'. They wanted to cash in on the housing boom. They scrambled to buy the cheap terraced houses. They tore out the Victorian interiors. They extended wherever the planners allowed them to extend. They installed kitchens with islands and bar stools and sliding picture windows. They laid new floors with handmade Italian tiles and oak parquet and deep-pile carpets in the bedrooms. They double-glazed and insulated. They transformed their back gardens with decking, lighting and ornamental trees. They modernised their front gardens, but not too ostentatiously. A question of taste.

In the summer, with the trees and flowerboxes in full bloom, Foxwood Road looked the picture of suburban tranquillity. Yet behind their plantation shutters, the residents seethed with anger and mutual recrimination. The hundred households were split by a proposal from the local council to make it a one-way street from the Common to the T-junction at the other end. The council said that modern society (or Foxwood Road, at least) could not function without deliveries. The one-way system would improve their flow.

Households that depended on deliveries liked the proposal. Their self-appointed leader was Fiona Bright, senior legal counsel for a well-known international accountancy firm and mother of three with a husband who worked for the National Trust. She lived at the Common end of the road. The anti-one-way proposal faction was led by Dorothy Smith-Mountain, who had a Doberman the size of a small pony. She was afraid of no one and her dog terrified dustmen, postmen and all other dog owners in the street. She liked a drink, but was mortified when told at the pub to leave her dog outside at the front for fear it would terrify infants and steal meat from the BBQ chef in the beer garden.

For some reason, families at opposite ends of the street held opposite views. People in the middle were moderate, undecided. And it was in the middle, at number twenty-nine, where the trouble began. The house had recently been sold to Mark and Kylie Stone. There was intense speculation by the curtain twitchers as to who they were.

They were never seen on the street. Rare glimpses of them in their garden (front and back) by inquisitive neighbours led to the conclusion that they were counter-culture; they looked like free thinkers exploring an alternative way of living because Mark was seen in a green silk shirt and Kylie wore hot pants. Their car had Welsh number plates, so someone said they might be druids. This was supported by the husband at number thirty-one, who said he had heard chanting coming from upstairs.

But what *most* upset the residents of Foxwood Road was the appearance of a gnome on a plinth in the Stone's front garden. The gnome was at the same height as pedestrians. It had a red hat, red nose and a white beard, and was smiling in the way that gnomes do.

The street was apoplectic. The Foxwood Road WhatsApp group carried expressions of anger even greater than those aroused by the one-way proposal. *'Outrageous'*; *'Need their heads examining'*; *'Who do they think they are?'*; *'An insult'*. But no one could produce a legal reason as to why they couldn't have a gnome in their front garden.

Fiona Bright suggested she should have a quiet word with the Stones under cover of lobbying in favour of the council proposal. The consultation period would end in three days' time. Fiona duly presented the council's case as a top lawyer would, ending with an emotional explanation of the importance of fast deliveries for families like hers. Then, she asked whether Mark and Kylie intended to keep the gnome where it was all year round. Or was it just a summer gnome? It seemed to be the only gnome in the area. Mark slammed the door.

Of her own accord, Dorothy Smith-Mountain also

thought she should lobby against the council proposal and raise the gnome issue. The very next day, accompanied by her huge dog, she rang the Stones' bell. Before the door opened, the dog growled at the gnome, waiting for it to show a sign of life. As it growled, it dribbled on the doorstep. Mark listened politely to the deep-voiced Dorothy. She said the council's plan was monstrous; two-way traffic was a democratic right; delivery vehicles had travelled for over a hundred years in both directions without problem. And on rubbish collection days, the pavements were obstructed and her dog needed to walk in the road without facing death from oncoming traffic. She wondered whether the gnome could sit on the ground. Mark said he was dealing with rather more important problems with his friends in Silicon Valley on the impact of artificial intelligence and wished her goodnight. He slammed the door so hard the knocker knocked.

Both Fiona and Dorothy claimed on WhatsApp that the Stones had got the message about the gnome. Their confidence was rudely shattered twenty-four hours later.

The gnome had been transformed. It had lights flashing in its eyes and turned in a circle every thirty seconds.

Fiona Bright sold up and left Clapham for Chelsea. Mrs Smith-Mountain's heart attack was said by the coroner to have been caused by stress.

THE BODYGUARD

Daniel Andoh's friends in the Metropolitan Police thought he was mad to take early retirement when he was doing so well. But they changed their tune when they heard of his cushy new job – British Ambassador's Protection Officer in Paris. They were jealous as hell. Until, that is, Daniel later told them that it meant being on duty every day, fourteen hours a day, with more danger per day than he'd had to deal with per week on average in the Met.

Daniel had done well in the police as a late entrant. He'd risen to sergeant in five years and was in line for promotion to inspector after ten. He was clever, strong and ambitious. He was Ghanaian, Ashanti to be precise, from central Ghana. His background was unique in the police force – for he was an illegal immigrant.

He'd excelled at school in Ghana despite terrible family problems. His father had, to put it politely, more than one wife, and when Daniel was eighteen, a family feud resulted in his mother being murdered. Daniel was the youngest child. He was traumatised by his mother's death, had nowhere to call home and decided to try his luck in Europe. His English was excellent. There were no jobs where he was, but the sale of his mother's jewellery raised the equivalent of $150. And he made useful money by carving lucky charms in wood, elephants especially, and selling his handiwork on the road. Elephants were associated with patience, wisdom, longevity and happiness, and were deeply revered.

Had he known how horrific his journey across the Sahara would be, how incredibly dangerous, he wouldn't have undertaken it. The frontiers he crossed meant little or nothing; it was the different tribes that mattered – Bambara, Fulani, Tuareg. The myriad armed groups all had different agendas. The militant Islamists – Boko Haram, Al-Qaeda – were the most scary and brutal. It took Daniel three months to get to Libya, which turned out to be the hardest, most racist and unfriendly place imaginable. He had better luck in Tunisia, especially the capital where people like himself found sanctuary in the cemetery of St George's Church. Daniel paid a fortune to reach the tiny island of Lampedusa. As he struggled through Italy and France to Calais, he was treated as an outcast, worse than an animal. It was no better in England, to start with. After five years of menial work and much help from charities and a Ghanian family in East London, the authorities allowed him to stay. How and why he was recruited by the police is an interesting story on its own.

Being black was both a hindrance and a help in the Met. There was racism and discrimination, but it also suited the top brass to protect and promote Daniel because it showed how inclusive they were. Ultimately, he became fed up with it all and when he saw the advertisement for the Paris job, he leapt at it.

His interview with the Foreign Office went well. His CV was so very different from the other candidates. His character references were outstanding; he had a firearms certificate and they liked the fact that he spoke French. The ambassador in Paris, Sir Archie Williams, was not involved in the selection, but soon realised how good Daniel was. Lady Williams got on with him very well, too.

Daniel had a tiny office adjoining the ambassador's private office and that of the social secretary. He actually spent many hours each week at a desk going through the ambassador's forthcoming engagements with a fine-tooth comb. Would there be trouble from students at the Sorbonne when he lectured there? Or at the England versus France football match? Was it safe to go for a walkabout in the suburb of Saint-Denis where cars were torched nearly every night and the police had stopped patrolling? And so on. Anglo-French relations had plummeted since Brexit; they were at their lowest ebb since de Gaulle vetoed the UK's application to join the Common Market in 1967. The ambassador was a high-profile target. It was his job to be high profile. Everyone knew where he lived, next to the Elysée Palace. Everyone knew he had a Rolls-Royce, which even flew a flag when he was travelling in it.

The French police used to share intelligence with the embassy about potential threats, places the ambassador should avoid, individuals who wished the British harm. There were plenty of them: nutcases with grudges; dual nationals who wrote in green ink (a sure sign of madness), furious the embassy wouldn't intervene with the authorities; animal welfare militants who thought the English were cruel to foxes. And so on. But since Brexit, this cooperation had ended. Daniel had to assess the threats himself with the help of others in the embassy, of course.

Every year in November, the ambassador marked Armistice Day by laying a wreath at a Commonwealth War Graves cemetery accompanied by his defence attaché. The cemetery, on the year of this story, was in Calais, where there were 943 graves, mostly British and immaculately kept. But the whole coast in the Pas-de-Calais department was a danger zone as far as Daniel was concerned because of militant fishermen. They had blockaded the ports; they had blockaded the approach road to the Channel Tunnel; and they had shown that they were not afraid to use violence. Harassing, insulting or attacking a British ambassador, or pouring paint over his Rolls-Royce would provide great publicity. The local police were unhelpful when Daniel rang them. So, he advised the ambassador not to go. This received a predictably negative response.

Daniel's worst fears were confirmed as the Rolls approached the cemetery gates. The Mayor of Calais was waiting behind crush barriers separating him from a group of about fifty angry fishermen with placards, saying. 'Save Our Jobs'. Three gendarmes looked on. But Daniel's eye was taken by a young man standing well apart from the fishermen, holding a football. He was wearing a thin denim jacket and looked cold. Daniel instantly recognised that he was Ashanti, surely Ghanaian, and most probably a migrant.

The young man kicked the football along the ground towards the ambassador's car. But the ball didn't roll, it zigzagged. Daniel shouted to the chauffeur to stop. He jumped out of the front seat, picked the ball up and hurled it to the grass verge on the other side of the road. The ball reeked of petrol. One of the gendarmes walked calmly towards the young man, but Daniel was there well beforehand. He signalled to the gendarme that he, Daniel, would handle this. No crime had been committed, he said.

Daniel towered over the young man, who looked scared.

"You're from Ghana, right?" he said in English.

"Yes," the young man said.

"Stupid thing to do, filling a good football with petrol, isn't it?"

"Yes."

Daniel looked the young man in the eyes for several seconds. He flashed back to his own time in Calais all those years ago. He walked towards the car, then turned back and held out his arm as if to shake hands. He pressed a fifty-euro note into the young man's hand, together with a little wooden elephant.

THE BENCH

Two older men, one short, one tall, shuffled and limped side by side towards a bench beside the bowling green on Clapham Common. The tall one was called Ian. He went all the way round the bench, suspiciously. The short one, called Ronald, made a big show of sweeping leaves from it with his copy of *The Times*. He then tore out the court page, folded it carefully in half, put it on one end of the bench and sat on it.

"*Lèse-majesté*, that is," said Ian. "Sitting on the court page is disrespectful to Her Majesty."

"Rubbish," said Ronald. "There's no photo of Her Majesty, God bless her. Would you like to sit on the obituaries page?"

"No thanks." Ian made himself comfortable at the other end of the bench, crossing his legs with an "Ahrgh" noise and half-turning towards Ronald.

When the two old friends realised that, for different health reasons, they needed to sit down, or thought they did, every ten minutes or so, they compiled a map of suitable benches around their houses – which were relatively close to each other. Competition to identify benches was understated but ever-present.

"Not a category one bench, this, Ronald. I'm surprised you put it on your list. There's a sad graffiti on the back."

"What does it say?"

"'*I love nobody and nobody loves me*'. Dated yesterday and signed 'Dorothy Smith'."

It was late morning in mid-September and the sun was out. Multitudes of mothers with babies in pushchairs occupied the other benches round the bowling green. Two Polish builders were taking an early lunch break on another bench while a small flock of pigeons waited for crumbs from their enormously thick sandwiches.

"That's not as bad as the graffiti on the bench by the Long Pond," said Ronald.

"What did that one say?" asked Ian.

"'*Dad died here. December 2019.*'"

"I'd been meaning to ask about your neighbour," said Ian.

"Which one?"

"Your learned friend. How's he getting on?"

"Left hospital last week. Back home now. What about *your* neighbour?" said Ronald.

"Last we heard, he was very sick. No longer see him in the back garden. Haven't even seen the district nurse going in and out any more."

Speech was impossible for a minute as a huge aircraft flew overhead on its way to land at Heathrow.

"I spoke to one of my old chums with Parkinson's

yesterday. Sounded frail. But he's found a live-in carer who's writing a book on sleep," said Ronald.

"Worth their weight in gold, live-in carers.," Ian continued. "Another friend down the road's got dementia. His wife had a major operation in April and she can't really cope without a live-in carer."

"It's hearts that worry me most," said Ronald.

"Me, too. I've a good friend in The Royal Brompton right now with an aneurysm in his aorta. And another chum in Dulwich who's still not right after a heart op in the summer. What about yourself, Ronald?"

"Mustn't complain." Ronald leant sideways and gently fished a small package from his coat pocket. It was beautifully wrapped with a blue ribbon. "Belgian chocolates. It's you-know-who's birthday today. Must remember to write a little card." He put the package back in his pocket.

Two young men with racquets, exuding good health, walked briskly in front of the bench towards the tennis courts.

"I dream of playing golf again," said Ian, wistfully.

"I've stopped myself from dreaming that dream," said Ronald, "because stuff would burst out of my back if I swung a club properly."

"On a positive note," said Ian, "have you noticed that the best educated children in the world are in Estonia? Every child goes to kindergarten at three. Children work electronically as a matter of course. Teachers can teach as they like and by fifteen, Estonian children outperform British children in every single subject."

"Even English?"

"Not sure about that. Probably."

"The problem in this country is discipline. Kids can't learn if there's backchat, rudeness between pupils, lack of respect for teachers and even the buildings. There have been three stabbings involving college students in the past five years – just round the corner from here."

"Yes. But that touches on the deep social problems we have. They have eliminated them in Estonia apparently. Teachers are expected to find ways of levelling-up pupils from all backgrounds within two years. Equality is in the Scandi-Finnish-Baltic culture."

"Why can't we have a culture like that? I can see our country moving closer to our Nordic neighbours as time goes on."

"First, we've got to sort out the mess of our relations with France," said Ian. "It beggars belief that in this day and age we should be insulting each other. We used to pride ourselves on our diplomacy and yet…"

From the side of the old pavilion, with the public toilets behind it and the busy café, came a lady wearing a light coat over a matching russet-coloured skirt and brown shoes. It was only when she was a few feet away from the bench that both men could see that her face was slightly disfigured, probably by a stroke. She stopped and, smiling, gestured at the space on the bench between the men. All the other benches were occupied.

"May I?" she said, pointing to the bench.

"Of course," both men said. "We were just going anyway."

"Oh. I was hoping to have a chat. Never mind." She sat down. She was carrying a large white envelope with her name on it in black, 'Dorothy Smith'.

As they got up to leave, both men clearly saw the name. Ronald drew the blue-ribboned package out of his coat pocket and gave it to her.

"Chocolates," he said.

THE QUEEN'S BIRTHDAY PARTY

O ther countries, ones with constitutions and national costumes, have national days and make a big fuss about them at home and abroad. The United Kingdom doesn't have a national day. Can you imagine the constituent nations of the UK ever agreeing on one? The Scots especially! It would be unthinkable. The union would fall apart.

Abroad, however, it would not do for every single other country to celebrate their national day, to beat their chests, to assert themselves in a competitive world, except the UK. So, we celebrate the Queen's Birthday with a reception instead. It's called the QBP in the jargon. It is always a splendid occasion. Climate permitting, it is often held in the residence garden in June. But any ambassador will tell you that celebrating the QBP is stressful, exhausting and fraught with diplomatic danger. There are booby traps for the unwary. Years of careful cultivation of an unfriendly minister or reclusive power behind the throne can be undone with a wrongly titled invitation envelope or a pork sausage canapé offered to a devout Muslim VIP.

Our story concerns one particular Queen's Birthday Party in a Muslim North African country just a few years ago. You will be relieved to hear it isn't about diplomacy and it isn't a send-up of diplomatic life. It isn't about the old democracies trying to outdo each other with the size of their respective receptions. Nor is it about the perceived slights of touchy celebrities who were not invited when they thought they should have been. It's about something more down to earth. It's about a gardener.

Months of preparation go into the QBP. Hundreds of embossed invitations are printed in the UK on stiff card with top-quality envelopes. Getting the guest list right is a major task. All parts of the embassy – political, commercial, aid, defence – make suggestions and the ambassador has the final say. Local British business sponsors for the event have to be found to swell the embassy's entertainment allowance. Seven hundred and fifty guests are invited – the foreign minister, the cabinet and the whole diplomatic corps – so car parking and security have to be carefully considered. Which members of staff should stand where in the garden? Where will the band play and for how long? What happens if it rains? But for the vital practical arrangements on the day – the lighting, the sound system, the servants, the drinks, the food, the loos – it is the ambassador's spouse who is responsible, who takes control.

This was the second time the ambassador had been posted here and his Arabic was fluent. But in between the two postings had come the so-called Arab Spring. That momentous upheaval in North Africa saw the end of the dictatorships, but also saw the emergence from the shadows of an ambitious, powerful, more radical, more conservative Islam. The ambassador was shocked to find how much it had appealed to the man in the street. The Islamists were in the ascendancy and it showed.

Even Malik, the head gardener at the residence, who had been there for thirty years, now prayed five times a day, whatever he was doing. His fasting at Ramadan was pitiless. He never failed to give coins to beggars. His most fervent wish was to make the pilgrimage to Mecca before he died. Jihad or battle against the infidel was probably impossible. But more insidious, perhaps, was a scarcely perceptible shift in attitude. Whereas before the revolution he was unquestionably loyal and respectful, he now regarded the British Embassy, his employer, with slight suspicion.

The residence garden was huge and deservedly famous. Half of it was an olive grove, which became a mass of wild flowers every spring. In the other half were different gardens divided by an avenue of stately palms and massive cypresses. There were peach, apricot, mulberry, almond and fig trees. Three dragon trees, a jacaranda and an enormous rubber tree provided colourful drama and gave shade to lawns, benches, a statue and a fountain. But above all there was a magnificent border designed and laid out by successive ambassadors' wives alongside the main lawn immediately behind the house. This was where the QBP was held. Irises, morning glory, hibiscus, geraniums, hollyhocks, poinsettia and lavender made a blaze of colour, attracting birds, butterflies and bees.

Good gardeners who knew how to cultivate flowers were as rare as gold dust. Malik stood out from the two other gardeners, who were basically of the slash and burn school: good at dealing with dead palm fronds, but not pricking out seedlings. They spent the middle of the day, when it was very hot, admittedly, sitting cross-legged in the shade of a honeysuckle-covered wall drinking mint tea. It was Malik's responsibility, overseen by the ambassador's wife, to have the main herbaceous border looking its best by the QBP in mid-June. It was his pride and joy. Herbaceous borders did not survive naturally in this part of the world. There was not enough rain for a start. So Malik fertilised, weeded, shaded and watered the flowers morning and evening. He had gone to immense trouble to have banks of sweet-smelling petunias almost touching the edge of the lawn.

This year, the ambassador wanted to celebrate his return to a country he loved. He and his wife had made a favourable impression on the people that mattered. They invited more than the place could cope with. There was an enormous turnout on the day. The party was for 6pm. By 6.30pm the lawn contained dozens of bunches of talking heads. By 6.45pm, the grass was invisible; guests were crammed together like commuters on the Northern Line. The waiters didn't have enough space to refill the glasses. The waitresses resorted to lifting their trays of canapés high above their heads to move around.

In return for a special bonus, Malik had been asked to patrol the garden during the reception. This, he did. But he was transfixed by what was about to happen to his herbaceous border, or so he feared. Cigarettes were being tossed into the hollyhocks; alcohol spilled over the hibiscus; but above all, his delicate petunias were in imminent danger of being trampled on.

Islam is a religion that promotes modesty and Malik's visits to the mosque had reinforced his belief in its importance. Everywhere he looked in his garden, he saw ladies being seductive. Most wore dresses which barely covered their knees. Many outfits were revealing and some even transparent. If he looked carefully, he could see underwear. Something flipped in Malik's mind. He felt he needed to react.

At 7.15pm, when it was already getting dark, the band stopped playing and the guests turned towards the spot at the edge of the lawn where it was clear the ambassador was about to say a few words. Malik had laid the wires for the microphone and an extra floodlight between the petunias and the grass. They led to a set of plugs connected to the garden's electricity circuit. They were held together by galvanised wire, so as to look neat. As the ambassador climbed the podium, Malik plugged the wires in and, with great strength, pulled them so that they were knee-height before plugging them in. He had created an electric fence to protect the herbaceous border. The ambassador's speech was interrupted by several squeals from ladies as they brushed their legs against the electric fence.

Malik smiled. He had performed his jihad.

TOUR DE FRANCE

The beautiful, wooded hills, ridges and deep valleys to the west of Lyon are full of history, jealousies – and cyclists. The Romans constructed four long aqueducts capturing the local spring water to supply their metropolis of Lugdunum (Lyon). The remains of these engineering marvels are still to be seen; sometimes in majestic arches striding across the landscape and sometimes in little heaps of bricks and cement in fields and villages. One such sad vestige stood beside the town hall of St Loup. More imposing aqueduct remains – two whole arches – lined the main street of St Jean-en-Haut, the neighbouring village on a parallel ridge five kilometres away, but divided from St Loup by a steep valley and six hundred years of enmity.

The trouble dated from the fourteenth century when St Loup was virtually exterminated by St Jean-en-Haut over a quarrel about holy relics. Relics meant pilgrims and pilgrims meant money. The villages still remained suspicious of each other centuries later. No one married outside the village. St Jean-en-Haut had six hundred inhabitants with only six surnames between them. Since the 1980s, it had had a police station, unlike St Loup. The Loupards never tired of saying they didn't need one. And for ten years running, thanks to judicious gift-giving by Maurice Gratiot, the mayor of St Jean-en-Haut, it had won the title of the prettiest, most flowery village in Les Monts du Lyonnais. A notice at both ends of the main street announced that the village was twinned with a village in Bavaria, famous for its edelweiss.

During the last war, an American aircraft crashed near St Loup and four men lost their lives. One of them, from the fabulously wealthy Kenton family, came from Wolf Point in Montana. His brother erected a monument at the crash site after the war and, with one thing leading to another, (not least that *loup* means wolf in English), St Loup became twinned with Wolf Point. The Kentons kept in regular touch to this day.

Mayor Gratiot thought it perfectly natural when the organisers of the Tour de France notified him that the next Tour would pass through St Jean-en-Haut. For the Tour de France to come through any city, town, village or hamlet meant prestige and big business benefits from the bakery to the town hall. The mayor let it be known that the decision was partly of his making, though in fact it was put to him as a *fait accompli*. Journalists from the world over would pass through. The mayor took a selfie of himself beside the aqueduct arch and posted it on Twitter and Facebook with the news of the Tour's appearance in the village. There would be extensive TV coverage by helicopter and motorbike of the cyclists swooping through the village. For forty-five minutes before the cyclists came, there would be 'the caravan': a procession of 150 vehicles, fifteen kilometres long – trucks carrying advertisements; radio stations advertising their wares with blaring pop music; open-topped lorries distributing T-shirts, baseball caps and sweets; open-topped luxury cars with pretty girls; motorbikes, ambulances, police cars. An unforgettable spectacle. Three and a half billion TV viewers would watch in 180 countries. The TV coverage would involve 260 camera people, thirty-five vehicles and six aircraft. The French government would cash in by unashamedly promoting tourism with brilliantly photographed film of the region in mid-summer – the local chateaux, the church and its relics; contented cows in unbelievably green pastures; and the local cheeses, of course. Amateur cyclists for years afterwards would ride the same routes as the professionals and be able to boast about it. The commercial spin-off was not negligeable. The village would be put on the map.

But Mayor Gratiot gave no thought at all to Madeleine Durier, the mayor of St Loup since last year. He had not spoken to her since her election. For one thing, the Durier family, all of whom had been successful farmers, had always been hostile to the Gratiots, who were unsuccessful farmers yet unbelievably arrogant. For another thing, Madeleine Durier was a woman. And thirdly, she was enormously popular. Maurice Gratiot decided he would never make the first approach. It was up to Madeleine Durier to do so. To say there was tension would not be an exaggeration. Both believed their village's respective sense of identity could best be maintained by denigrating the other.

When Madeleine Durier heard that the Tour de France

would go through St Jean-en-Haut, her first thought was that this was grossly unfair. So did the municipal council. She needed little urging to ask the Tour organisers to reroute the race through St Loup. It would shorten that day's 225-kilometre 'stage' by one kilometre, which was nothing. For a tortured night, she considered various stratagems – sabotage of the bridge just outside St Jean; fake news emanating from Maurice Gratiot about the Tour's carbon footprint; or that the pollution caused by the Tour caravan would kill St Jean's flowers. As she looked out of her mayoral office window at the pathetic pile of bricks that were said to be aqueduct remains, Madeleine Durier came up with an idea – high risk, but surely highly attractive to the organisers. Above all, it would infuriate Gratiot.

First, Madeleine Durier had to do some quick research. The Tour de France was run by a private company that kept its accounts secret. But it existed to make money. Towns pay the company to be included on the route. But prize money for the riders is relatively small by the standards of today's professional sport.

Obtaining an interview with the Tour planners was not easy. Madeleine had an instinctive antipathy to anything based in Paris ('Parisian' was almost an insult to some of the older folk in St Loup). But she was pretty and witty, with a husky voice on the phone that opened most doors. The stakes were high. She was prepared to push aside her dislike of Paris for the sake of bringing the Tour to St Loup.

Come the day, she was surprised that there were only men in the room where she had to make her illustrated presentation. No women. She gave the performance of her life. It was early autumn and a lucky sunbeam lit up her shining auburn hair. She was wearing a tartan waistcoat over a cream silk shirt with the collar up. Her tartan skirt, fastened with a silver safety pin, revealed a perfect pair of legs. The suited executives had fallen for her charms long before her final pitch and summing up.

"St Loup's history – its religious relics, its bubbling springs, its quaint houses, its long, flat main street and its unique *art de vivre* – make it a natural setting for that part of the Tour. St Loup has never been privileged in the past to host the Tour. We think our time has come." She paused and met the gaze of each of the men one by one.

"What we are offering is a 100,000 euros purse for the first rider to reach the town hall. We could call it the Aqueduct Assignment or the St Loup Sprint." The finance director nodded, then laughed, then nodded again. The rest of the room rocked with pleasure. The suits said they hadn't heard a word from St Jean-en-Haut and they certainly hadn't had a commercial proposition like they had just had from St Loup. The finance director was not quite finished, however.

"Where will your 100,000 euros come from, Madame Mayor?"

"From public subscription and a generous gift from a US benefactor. When my village heard we could poke St Jean in the eye this way, we were actually oversubscribed."

THE REVOLUTION

C hauffeurs working for the President were hand-picked, security-vetted and well paid. Ahmed Laroui was the youngest and obtained the job through his father, Hedi, an ex-military acquaintance of the President. Hedi was now Director of the airport. As the most junior driver, Ahmed had to drive the Ford Transit van that was used for all the unglamourous work – collecting shopping for the President's extravagant wife, distributing gifts and transferring or collecting baggage. The Laroui family had watched their beloved North African country slide from parliamentary democracy to dictatorship in the space of just a few years. But they said nothing and did nothing for fear of losing their jobs. And jobs were extremely hard to find.

Not that the President was aware of that. The unemployment figures he was shown were massively falsified. The President lived in la-la land, a fantasy world where no one dared tell the truth. Had the President spent a day shopping or queuing at the bank or at the petrol station? Indeed, if he had just walked downtown, he would have had a shock. There were often shortages of basic foods; prices went up every day; beggars multiplied; thousands of young men lounged around doing nothing. But the President never saw this.

Before he was driven to a function, the brown grass on both sides of the road was sprayed green and the kerbstones were whitewashed. The citizens he met had been told what to say. And everywhere he looked he saw his own portrait, part of a personality cult which underpinned his megalomania.

He was maintained in power by an enormous security apparatus led by the Minister of the Interior. Dissent was brutally repressed. The press and broadcasting were closely controlled; the internet shut down if necessary. A fake opposition party was allowed – indeed, supported – by the president as pathetic proof to the outside world that the country was a democracy. When citizens were caught using social media to publicise regime scandals, they were given prison sentences long enough to act as a deterrent to any others following in their footsteps.

Ahmed's work driving a van kept him in touch with the real world outside the palace gates. So did his extended family. One brother was an olive farmer, another brother a teacher, and a sister worked as a receptionist in a hospital. Trusting in Ahmed's discretion, they told him regularly of how the police were hated; of the true, verified stories of the President's corruption that disgusted everyone. Ahmed's father was as well aware as his children of the fast-rising anger throughout the country. The huge portraits of the President at the airport were being regularly defaced.

The revolution was triggered by the arrest of a tv

celebrity for daring to suggest that today everything had a price. With a bribe, in other words, nothing was impossible. The unlucky man was held in a cell underneath the Ministry of the Interior. The word went round the capital like wildfire that there would be a protest outside the ministry after midday prayers on Friday, when the streets were legitimately full of people. And the white ihram clothing worn on Fridays could conceal things.

About an hour after the mosques had emptied, the centre of town was in ferment. Thousands upon thousands, the people poured out of side streets and moved towards the Interior Ministry. It seemed to have been caught off guard because there were only some hundred or so police at the bottom of the steps leading to the front door. The worst of insults were shouted at them for a good half hour. It emerged later that they had been told they could fire into the crowd if their lives were threatened. Significantly, they didn't use their weapons at all. There was huge excitement in the air and much tension. But this was the moment people, including Ahmed and Hedi, had been dreaming of. When everyone saw how many they were together in the streets, their courage increased. A believable rumour went round that the army would be called in. But even that fear was forgotten when the police – slowly at first, then in a rush – laid their weapons down in a pile on the pavement and walked into the outstretched arms of the protesters. Within minutes, the huge crowd started the five-mile walk to the President's palace.

The first indication Ahmed had of what was happening was when the President's private secretary threw open a window and shouted to Ahmed to bring his van to the staff entrance and to be ready to load baggage. Orders came in all directions to the other drivers and army guards to prepare first this vehicle, then a different one. The chief of staff was seen running from one part of the building to another. "They'll be here in forty-five minutes," he shouted. "The President will leave in ten minutes." He saw Ahmed beside the van and told him to collect the President's bags from the first floor. Quickly.

Inside the palace, there was panic such as he had never seen before. All of the fireplaces were being used to burn documents. After Ahmed had loaded six Gucci suitcases into the van, the chief of staff himself struggled to lift and load a black tin box with handles on both sides and the initials BC beside the keyhole on the front.

"Weapons?" Ahmed was bold enough to ask.

"Gold – much heavier," came the reply. "Get it in the plane with the President's bags or your life won't be worth living, understand?" Ahmed slammed the van door shut and locked it before putting the padlock on the metal bar holding both doors tightly in place.

"Understood. I'll phone my father at the airport."

"OK. But he knows we're coming."

In the presidential convoys, Ahmed's van usually followed the ambulance and preceded the last security car but he could see that this convoy was going to be very short, indeed as inconspicuous as possible. Ahmed ran to a spot behind the garage where he knew he couldn't be seen or above all heard.

He called his father on his personal mobile. "Black tin box with Banque Centrale or BC – no, just the initials 'BC' – beside the keyhole. My black tin box of tools is beside it in the van. Six suitcases." No more needed to be said.

The President was driven to the airport in a yellow saloon car, looking exactly like one of the thousands of taxis in the capital. He was followed by just one security Mercedes and Ahmed was in third place.

The scene around the President's personal plane was one of intense simulated activity. On one side of the cargo door was a food truck with its platform elevated and laden with plastic-covered boxes. On the other side was a mobile airport generator with huge wheels. Two high-sided airport maintenance trucks with flashing red lights made space for Ahmed's Transit van, which reversed to the cargo hold. As the van arrived, so did Ahmed's father in an airport pick-up, also with blue lights flashing. He ordered the half dozen overalled staff to go back to the VIP gates beside the terminal while he personally supervised the loading. Father and son pulled the Gucci suitcases out of the van and into the cargo hold. They heaved the black tin box of tools with a crash into the hold. And they carefully lifted the Banque Centrale box into the airport director's pick-up. Five minutes later, the President was airborne and headed for exile. One hour later, five million dollars in gold bars were returned to the Central Bank where they belonged.

THE BARBER

B arber shops only a few years ago were rare male preserves, islands of testosterone, with girlie magazines and smutty jokes. Clients pretended to be on intimate terms with the barbers and talked to other clients without need of introduction. As at the bar in the pub, one could talk breezily to complete strangers. It's all changing now. The magazines have gone. One might easily have one's hair cut – very well – by Christina or Maya. And they don't do jokes.

At the time of this story, five years ago, Dmitri, British born, had been running an establishment in Clapham with his father, Cyprus born, for twenty-five years. They were unfailingly polite. Clients became friends. They were flattered and pampered, complimented, never shamed. A shampoo was accompanied by an amazing scalp massage. Dimitri had a good sense of humour. The price list above the mirror ended with 'OAPs – *reduced price Tuesdays. Lottery winners pay double'*. Clients left feeling better all round.

Dimitri's dad was still working there at eighty-two. He was cutting a doctor's hair when the doctor noticed the old man's eye was drooping and he was slurring his words. The doctor got out of the chair, took out his phone and dialled 999 for an ambulance. They both went to A&E where it was quickly discovered the barber had had a stroke. He recovered – and a month later, returned to work!

Dimitri was once cutting my hair two days before Christmas at about three in the afternoon. Dmitri said, "See that guy lounging outside the window? He's a client of mine. He's a criminal. He told me, quite proudly, he steals a turkey from the Sainsbury's Local each Christmas. He waits till the shop is crowded, nips in and puts a turkey in his backpack. He's out and down the underground before you can say 'knife'."

Dimitri was a keen observer of the social scene. His intelligence constantly surprised me. He had wanted to go to university and become a doctor, but his family didn't support him. On the contrary, his parents insisted he should join his dad's business and earn money. He married a girl from school, who later became a solicitor. Their son was a very talented musician.

Dimitri's talent was his handling of people of all sorts. He would patiently help the long-time client, who now had Alzheimer's, with the story he'd told Dimitri a dozen times already, of how he had sailed his yacht round the Baltic. He would nod agreement to the youths who came in wanting an undercut, a quiff or spikes. I even heard him say "No problem" to the cool fifteen-year-old who said he wanted his hair messy.

Saturdays were always interesting, he told me. He visited a private client first thing Saturdays. I thought he was joking when he said this man had his own barber's chair in his basement. He never said his name. He was far too discreet. The Saturday afternoon shift, in the old days, was difficult because of the drunks coming from the pub down the road. They came to sober up with a cold-water shampoo. If they'd just seen their team lose on the telly, the football fans would use foul language. Worst of all, they would vomit in the basin. Rugby fans were better behaved.

The barber's chair in the basement was the clue that told me the private client's name – Sir Martin Harz. I had met him at a Save Clapham Common garden party years earlier. We were talking about the fashion for digging basements under our terraced houses to make TV or playrooms. A house nearby had just collapsed as the excavation was proceeding. Sir Martin said basements were useful; he had a barber's chair in his.

I later discovered that the middle-aged, silver-haired Sir Martin was actually a billionaire – the only one I'd met. It was thrilling that he should live in our neighbourhood. He was happily married with three children, kept a very low profile and passed unrecognised in the street. Not that he went out that much. He did not need to jog, for example, because he had a fully equipped gym and a swimming pool also in his basement. He had given very few interviews. My information came from another source. He was an extraordinarily generous philanthropist. Although he had made very large donations to museums, art galleries (plural) and his old university, he found more satisfaction in helping smaller charities or organisations.

Sir Martin was a disillusioned political donor. He had hoped the party he supported would have kept the UK in Europe, but in the end, it wasn't the parties that decided the outcome. He was unhappy that he hadn't predicted it. Since the referendum, he had decided to inform himself more closely with public opinion. One of many ways to do this was to listen to his barber, Dimitri.

Dimitri's regulars included journalists from both sides of the political spectrum; second-generation immigrants, especially Greeks; young professionals who lived locally; teachers; and the owner of a bookshop, called James. Dimitri had known James for ten years at least. He never knew his family name, but then that was true of most of his clients. The two men were on the same wavelength. They both loved reading and books generally. And they both loved spy stories. There was nothing they didn't know, so they thought, about MI5 and MI6, for instance.

James was usually upbeat and cheerful, with his experiences of bizarre clients, of peculiar reading habits – "*Sodomy in the Vatican*? Yes, vicar. We can have that here by the end of the week." Experiences that matched Dimitri's, quirk for quirk.

But Dimitri could tell one Friday evening, just before closing actually, that James was not well. The sinews in his neck and shoulders were as tense as tightropes. He hadn't shaved. There were creases round his eyes. And grey hairs that hadn't been there before.

Dimitri was discreet; an understanding confidante. The two were alone. James let it all come out. He needed to talk to someone.

The fact was, James said, that that there was no place for independent bookshops any longer. His had a good location with a decent footfall; he was surrounded by excellent schools; people in the area were amongst the highest earners in the country. He'd refreshed his window every week. He'd increased his offerings of greetings cards. He'd tried discounts and sales. He'd had wine and cheese evenings with authors. He'd increased his stock in cookery, self-help, childcare, box sets, fitness and children's. To no avail.

Business had slowly and painfully disappeared. Perhaps people were reading less, were too busy with their phones, were using e-books. Business rates were astronomical. Above all, he couldn't compete with Amazon and their next-day delivery. He'd worked his socks off trying to keep the business afloat. He was exhausted.

James slumped in the chair. Dimitri turned the sign on the door to closed. They talked for another ten minutes and James left, despondent but glad that he'd got it off his chest.

The following Monday, at the bookshop, a middle-aged man with silver hair asked for James by name, gave him an envelope and quietly left.

It contained a cheque for £100,000.

THE DEAL

Viewed from a drone, the north bank of the mighty Thames between Dagenham and Southend is not something God would be proud of. The land is flat and marshy. Tilbury Docks is the beating heart, still our biggest port, and for miles east and west there is a twentieth-century soulless industrial landscape that Americans would recognise – refineries, warehouses, lorry parks, power stations, factories and tens of thousands of cheap houses.

This was Wade Park School's environment. The 1960s buildings were no longer fit for purpose in 2018. It was desperately understaffed. Thirty teachers tried their best to equip their one thousand disadvantaged pupils for life outside. It was hard going.

Andrew Eland had spent the first ten years of his teaching career in Dagenham – no longer the town it used to be since Ford downsized twenty years ago. He taught English and football. He wanted a change, was up for a challenge and was accepted at Wade Park after a five-minute interview.

All things considered, the school hadn't done badly in

the past couple of years. But Year 9 (13-14-year-olds), to which Andrew was assigned at the start of the new school year in September, was a different story according to the principal. Class C in Year 9, Andrew's class, had gone backwards.

After just one day, it became apparent where the problem was. Marco Fraser, a taller-than-average youth with a loud and foul mouth. Marco was constantly combing his oiled black hair during lessons. His hairstyle was modelled on Ronaldo, footballer of the year. Marco wasted no time in testing the new teacher by holding his new English textbook upside down and making the class laugh. Andrew was patient at first – a mistake, thinking that the twenty-nine others in the class would eventually prefer to learn something rather than nothing. He thought Marco would calm down, would respond to reason. The very first thing Andrew ordered Marco to do was to call him 'sir', to teach him respect. It was slow work.

As the days passed, it became clear the youth was out of control. He thrived on playing the fool, on interrupting, on making the girls giggle. He never sat still; he clicked his biro in and out until it broke; he blew bubbles with his bubble gum until the bubbles exploded. The pity was that Marco was not mentally deficient. Very occasionally, he said something surprisingly sensible. He brought climate change home to the class when he said that if sea levels continued to rise, Dagenham would soon be flooded.

Of course, Andrew discussed the Marco problem in the staffroom with his other teachers. Some thought he was simply too disruptive and ought to be removed from the school. That would mark him for life. Some thought he should be sent out of the classroom every time he misbehaved. He would probably disappear for the day. But Andrew said he wanted to try something else. Because he had seen him playing football.

On the football pitch, he saw Marco was gifted with a swerve and a turn of speed that was rare. He dribbled and sidestepped mesmerically. His ball control was quite exceptional for a fourteen-year-old. But he ruined it all by not passing to teammates and by clowning around when he scored a goal (which he always did).

As luck would have it, Andrew had a friend, David, from his sports training/college days who now worked as a talent scout. Andrew phoned him after he had seen Marco playing half a dozen times. David duly drove out at Andrew's invitation to watch Marco unobtrusively from the comfort of his car one October afternoon. Within half an hour, David had seen enough. The youth had great gifts.

That same evening, David phoned Andrew. It was a long call. David said he would like to meet Marco and his mother. But there was more emphasis than ever these days on boys continuing schoolwork at the same time as learning how to play professional football.

"How is Marco's schoolwork?" asked David.

Andrew hesitated, then took a risk by saying, "He's very far from stupid, but he won't concentrate in the classroom so his academic achievements so far are not great, to be honest."

"Well, the academy won't take him unless you can assure me that he will pass his GCSEs in English and maths," Alan said.

"Leave it with me for twenty-four hours," said Andrew.

As the bell sounded for the lunch break the next day, Andrew ordered Marco to stay behind for a word.

"Sit down in front of my desk, Marco. And wipe that smirk off your face." There was a pause while the two looked at each other. "I asked a friend to watch you playing football yesterday afternoon because I think you're good. He rang me up at home last night. He said you were not bad, but that you showed off all the time and you talked back to the referee. It's true. You show no respect. He said you were emotionally immature. Do you know what 'emotionally immature' means, Marco? It means you're not grown up; that you think it's funny to play the fool all the time; that what happens in the classroom is not important. My friend was absolutely right. You don't behave like the young adult you are. Your attitude to work is unworthy of you. It's pathetic. And it's infecting the whole class. I'm not having it any longer."

Marco had never been spoken to like this. He looked at the floor.

"I can help you make something of your life, Marco, if, only if, you change your whole attitude. Do you want me to help you? Do you?"

Another long pause.

"Yes," Marco whispered.

"My friend is a talent scout. He liked what he saw of your football. He would have to talk to your mum about his club's youth academy. But first he has to have an assurance in writing from me that you will pass your GCSEs in English and maths next year."

Marco looked up from the floor, sat up straight and was speechless.

"So, here's the deal," Andrew said. "I'll send him an assurance in writing only if you change your behaviour – towards me, towards the class and the school. No more fooling around. You focus on schoolwork to the exclusion of all else. By the way, the club is Arsenal. What do you say?"

Marco dipped his head because he didn't want Andrew to see that his eyes were glistening. He was pleased beyond words.

"Arsenal? Cool." For the first time, Marco looked Andrew in the eye. "I'm on for the deal. Yes."

"Yes, what?"

"Yes, *sir*."

They high-fived.

TREE POWER

In the nineteenth century, one of the attractions of the Isle of Wight for aristocratic German families was the presence at Osborne House of Prince Albert of Saxe-Coburg-Gotha, Queen Victoria's brilliant consort. For some time after Prince Albert's tragic death in 1861, when he was only forty-two years old, German families continued to come for the summer especially. Dr Otto Fischer and his wife, Martha, had already been twice, renting houses in Cowes, then Yarmouth and, finally, in the summer of 1875, at Martha's insistence, Freshwater Bay.

Dr Fischer, a mathematician by training, liked the Isle of Wight because there was little light or smoke pollution and he could indulge his passion for astronomy. He had built his own telescope, which had to be carefully packed in a special crate, transported from Munich and then unpacked each year. His interest was in examining the newly found minor planets and he maintained a learned correspondence with the Berlin and Greenwich Observatories. The Fischers had five children, which utterly amazed their friends, for they always seemed to be quarrelling. Martha was an outspoken free-thinker, a believer in bloodletting using leeches, and suspicious of mathematics. She believed in reincarnation, that we could return as an animate or inanimate being. While Otto was a stereotypical scientist who wanted to know what was on the dark side of the moon, Martha was a romantic who felt the moon's influence in her body once a month. She communed with nature in her native Black Forest in dozens of ways: picnics in woodland glades, garlands she made for the children, songs and carols, maypoles, Green Men. Otto ridiculed her tree worship. Why should oaks be sacred? What was so special about yew or hazel or mistletoe, for that matter? Martha said hazel had magical powers. She said she drew strength from ancient forests. Otto once called her a pagan to her face.

Martha's yearning for a spiritual and romantic dimension to life led her to the poetry and the person of Alfred Tennyson. The mystical, visionary and fantasy aspects of his verse spoke to her soul. He lived at Farringford House in Freshwater, just the sort of spacious, ivy-covered abode with gothic embellishments that she expected the poet laureate to live in. It seemed right that the national poet should live close to his sovereign, or 'Mrs Brown', as the Queen was called by her adoring subjects.

Otto and Martha's days were not synchronised. Otto worked at night with his telescope and slept until mid-morning while Martha liked to be outdoors straight after breakfast. Martha's walks usually took her to the spectacular down behind Farringford House where, more often than not, she would accidentally bump into Tennyson himself. There were always mutual acknowledgements even though they had never been introduced. Martha's "Good day, Lord Tennyson" was met with a touching of the hat by the prince of literature, who, without breaking his stride, would smile, make a half-turn and say, "Good day, Madam." Every glimpse of the poet laureate was recorded by Martha in her diary. She was by no means Tennyson's only admirer. Indeed, the reason he had to abandon his life at Farringford House, at least in the summer months, was because he was stalked by too many star-struck tourists.

Martha noticed every detail of the great man's behaviour, who he was with and his wardrobe. She particularly noticed his walking stick and the way he swung it rhythmically like a drum major. She learnt from the vicar's wife at All Saints and St Agnes that he had bought the stick from a shop in Yarmouth just four miles away.

So it was that for Otto's birthday on the fourth of August, Martha found herself in George Pittis' shop in Yarmouth. Her heart skipped a beat when the shop assistant pointed to a discreet sign in the corner of the shop window – "By Appointment to Her Gracious Majesty Queen Victoria, walking stick makers." Her expression of surprise caused George Pittis himself to come out of his workshop, brushing wood shavings off his jacket. He sensed a sale to the lady with a German accent. He had a very distinct Isle of Wight accent himself.

"They say – mind, I can't tell how true it is – that our dear Queen favours two sticks. One, made of oak, came down to her from Charles the Second. Oak is that strong, it is. But she found the gold handle uncomfortable and changed it for an ivory one. The other stick she favours, I'm proud to say," and here George Pittis puffed out his chest a fraction, "is mine. Made of hazelwood. Magical powers, has hazelwood. Wards off evil spirits and brings good luck." He picked one out of a long rack, ran one hand over its length and handle, and gave it to Martha. She held it across her chest like a sceptre.

"Is it for yourself, Madam?"

"No, for my husband's birthday." She looked bemused at the fantastic assortment of sticks and their labels – white beech, ash, blackthorn, oak and ebony. Her gaze settled on a highly polished one with a splendid carved handle.

"In the Italian style, Madam. But it's chestnut, a wood brought here by the Romans, not really a native tree. The hazel would suit better, I think. It's my belief that each wood has a personality."

"I couldn't agree more, Mr Pittis. May I be indiscreet and ask which one Alfred Tennyson chose?"

"More than my reputation is worth, Madam." But George Pittis' smile showed the flattery had worked. He paused, then said in a clear voice, "The hazel."

The fourth of August was marked by a gale of rare intensity. On presenting Otto his hazel stick, Martha said it was like a magician's wand.

"Nonsense, my dear," Otto said.

"I believe it has supernatural powers," Martha bravely said.

"Fiddlesticks, my dear. But after a storm like this, the sky will be wondrously clear for my telescope tonight."

The wind was still blowing in from the Channel at 10pm, howling through the cedar of Lebanon on one side of the house and swishing at the laurel bushes along the drive. Otto's telescope, on its tripod, was firmly planted on the lawn behind the servant's entrance. There was less light from the house there at night. His routine was always the same. He drew up a chair close to the telescope's eyepiece, took off his hat, opened his notebook and slowly focused the lens. This time, he placed his walking stick beside his hat on the grass and as he straightened himself in the chair, there was a furious gust of wind followed by a rumbling, rolling noise, then a whoosh – and a chimney pot smashed onto his top hat, shattering into a hundred pieces, knocking the telescope over. Otto went rigid with fright and shock. He fully expected to see blood from his legs at the very least. But there was none. He was unharmed.

A minute later, Martha came running out of the back door in her night clothes. She saw her husband was unhurt, embraced him as he stood up, picked up the walking stick lovingly and said to herself, "Hazel. I knew it. The power of wood."

BEAVER LAKE

Beaver Lake is as well known to Montrealers as the Serpentine is to Londoners. It's a rather small, clover-shaped, artificial lake sitting near the top of Mount Royal, from which Montreal takes its name. It's the symbol of the city and on one of the mountain's three peaks is a giant illuminated cross. In winter, just after a snowfall, trekking up to Beaver Lake is exhilarating, even awe-inspiring. The trails through the park follow the contours of the Mountain through the pine and maple woods that surround it. The snow can be deep and crunches satisfyingly under one's skis as one pushes upwards. Slabs of snow slide off the pine branches onto the trail when stirred by a breeze or warmed by the sun. The crystals glisten and twinkle when waving ski-tips dip into the fresh powder. The cold air smells of resin and newly washed sheets. The only noise is made by one's slippery skis or black, wing-flapping crows.

On arrival at the lake, there is more noise, this time from skaters. With one's own skates, it's free and far bigger than any artificial rink. There's a spirit of freedom and companionship, of fun, good humour and romance – the essence of Canada.

Lorraine Clement's anthropology course at McGill University at the foot of The Mountain was always oversubscribed. It was widely acknowledged that she had turned what had been a rather dry study of man as an animal into an inspirational course focusing more on the psychology of the human race – of why we behave as we do. She chose to teach in English. Her husband Marc, however, had to teach his neuroscience students at l'Université de Montréal, one mile away, in French. The couple liked to think, wishfully, that their slightly unusual anglophone/ francophone marriage was a sign of the beginning of the end of the language dispute in Quebec. What was certain was that their disciplines were complementary. There was a spin-off from his work to hers and vice versa.

Lorraine and Marc were both absorbed by their academic careers. She was forty and he was forty-two when they had met at Beaver Lake's snack bar, having laughed at each other on the ice while trying to skate backwards. It was love at first sight with a cerebral dimension. They wanted children, but it was Marc who said they had probably missed the biological bus. It sounds peculiar, but unconsciously they both shifted the affection they would have given their own children onto other young people. Perhaps that's what made them outstanding teachers. But their childlessness was also an unspoken sadness.

Lorraine was super conscientious about her students. Despite outward appearances – wispy beards for boys, tight waists and minis for girls – the students were often emotionally immature, unsure of themselves and vulnerable. Lorraine wondered whether the social media generation's obsession with celebrities, role models and the need to keep constantly in touch with peers was actually a sign of the generation's insecurity.

Lorraine had noticed Andrea from the first days of the academic year. She had a withered arm, the result of polio, and turned up to classes wearing too much make-up and too much scent. She never smiled. No one wanted to sit next to her. Her work was good and she was undoubtedly intelligent. The communal bonding, flirting and excitement of a first semester at McGill completely passed her by. Her loneliness was cruelly evident.

At the end of Lorraine's last lecture on patterns of behaviour, Andrea hung back as the other students filed out for lunch into the first decent snowfall of the winter. The lecture hall was empty. As Andrea slowly packed her things away into a satchel, she looked up several times at Lorraine, who could feel they needed to talk.

"Are you enjoying social anthropology, Andrea? I really liked your essay last week; you've been reading widely. Well done."

"Thank you," said Andrea. "Reading is all I've got to do. It's quiet at home because Dad's abroad and Mum's at work till late." She looked at Lorraine squarely for the first time. The corners of her mouth were down. "The others seem to be having so much fun. There must be something wrong with me," she said, holding up her withered arm. "I don't know…" She was desperately holding back tears.

She stood up and looked out of the window. The fresh snow had softened all the contours on the campus. Little puffs of snow were blowing off the hat and coat of the statue of James McGill. A girl squealed with laughter as a broad-shouldered boy with a Davy Crockett fur hat landed a snowball on her. It gave him the chance to offer to brush the snow off her. But before he could do so, she scored a direct hit on him. And they both laughed.

"There's absolutely nothing wrong with you, Andrea. We need to get you socialising, that's all. I had the same problem as you because I became too wrapped up in my work. I didn't think about boys enough – until too late, really."

A flicker of a smile crossed Andrea's face for the first time.

"I've got a cunning plan. Do you skate?" Lorraine asked.

"Yes. I love it, but lacing up my skates with one hand is difficult."

"Saturdays, there's always a young crowd skating on Beaver Lake. I met my husband there, in the snack bar." Andrea looked interested. "Meet me outside the changing cabin there at eleven on Saturday with your skates. I'll have mine in my backpack because I'll be on skis. Skiing on the Mountain is my weekend exercise. Oh. A word of friendly advice: no make-up and no perfume."

Lorraine later wondered whether she was right to get so involved with a student. But she reasoned that as staff, she had a welfare role. The year before, there had been a tragic case of a lonely boy committing suicide at McGill. Elite universities were sink or swim places. Lorraine so much hoped she could help Andrea swim.

Saturday morning was one of those brilliant winter days in Quebec. The thermometer showed minus five degrees, but the sun blazed in a cloudless royal blue sky.

The snow had a thin crust like the sugar on a *crème brûlée*. Lorraine's breath ballooned in the freezing air as steam does from a boiling kettle. Her lips tingled as she skied up the Mountain.

It was a nervous but excited Andrea who was waiting for Lorraine outside the cabin changing room. There were pretty dimples at either side of her wide smile. Her blue eyes glittered like sapphires. She had her skates on and was chatting to a knockout handsome young man in a red sweater and red hat.

"Hi, Lorraine. This is Robin. He helped me lace up my skates."

"Great. Hi, both of you. I'll be out in five minutes," said Lorraine.

When Lorraine reappeared, she couldn't believe her eyes. Andrea and Robin were skating hand in hand. They were both laughing.

"See you in the snack bar," Andrea said, winking.

Lorraine smiled.

ALWAYS BELIEVE

She'd been away for a month exactly. Her doctor had said she badly needed a break, a change of scene, some sunshine perhaps, after all she'd been through. Mary should have expected it to be pouring with rain when the taxi stopped at the front gate; it was November, after all. She had been holding the little key to her mailbox on her front gate since she had settled in the taxi. One quick turn of the key and she had all the post in her hands. She rapidly flipped the envelopes over each other, but of course didn't find what she wanted.

She sighed then took a deep breath. She saw that the dustmen had left the gate open again, despite her having told them to close it more than once. This time yesterday in Morocco, she had been looking at oranges dropping off the trees. Now, a day later, here in Bournemouth, leaves littered the lawn and the first Channel gale had brought the remaining conkers down, cluttering the garage gutters. She remembered how, years ago, it was impossible to stop kids climbing over the fence and squashing the spikey capsules till their slippery contents spun out. That is, as long as her Philip hadn't beaten them to it.

It was the same with the apples in the orchard at the back of the house. If boys were brave enough to cross the brambles, climb the fence and pocket a few apples, Mary didn't mind. Philip had usually picked all the two of them needed anyway.

As she pulled her old suitcase round the drive to the front door, Mary told herself she felt much better. She'd have to get used to being on her own. She instinctively avoided the puddles below the front step. Philip, her son, always said he would dig a little drain there to solve the problem, but he never did. He said he couldn't match his father's legendary house maintenance skills, so he didn't try. Ever since her husband Tom's death eight years ago, Mary had had to struggle to keep the old farmhouse going. And since Philip's disappearance two years ago, Mary had lost heart – had pretty much given up. *What was the point?* she kept asking herself. She had managed to come to terms with Tom's death after just a few months because there had been Philip to look after. Philip was her reason for living.

She put the post down on the hall table, switched on the lights and was about to turn up the thermostat until she remembered she had to turn on the boiler in the boiler house first. Back in the kitchen, she noticed the cold tap was dripping. It hadn't been fully turned off. Had it been dripping for a month?

It had been great to have had Philip around the house after Tom died. There was an emptiness otherwise. She felt more comfortable, more normal, better protected. Little things in the old house triggered memories, always good ones; bad memories were consigned to the back of the brain. As she hung up her raincoat, she recalled for a second that she and Tom had bought the coat stand at an antique shop in Chichester, only to find that it wouldn't fit in their tiny car. They drove to Bournemouth with it sticking out of the window. Then, there was the sofa that she should have recovered years ago. For Philip, settling on the sofa to watch rugby on TV frequently had brought on happy thoughts of Dad next to him, with a can of beer and a packet of crisps. Tom's enthusiasm was infectious, shouting when a try was scored or a foul was missed by the referee.

Tom's importance for Mary was deep and complex. They needed each other emotionally. More than once, Mary had been described as having a nervous disposition. She was highly strung. She was easily excited. Tom was always calm – except when watching sport – and extraordinarily patient. He believed in the United Nations and wild swimming. What Tom meant for Mary was a loving friendship, mutual understanding, a childlike pleasure in surprises, and humour.

When Philip turned eighteen, he'd been fatherless for four years. Mary did her best to make up for it by encouraging Philip to enjoy male company out of school – winter weekends of cyclo-cross using a club bike in the Surrey Hills; summer sea-fishing with neighbours; and metal-detecting all year round. In his last year at school, Philip decided he wanted to be a doctor, a GP. His mother liked the idea and she knew Tom would have approved. Mary never said so, but she hated the idea that her son would have to leave home for years of medical training.

She knew she had to stop thinking about all that. She flopped down on the armchair in front of the blank TV screen. If her GP had thought that a month's holiday would make her forget everything, he was wrong. Philip had disappeared. Or rather he was – in police parlance – a missing person. When the police told Mary after eighteen months that they were going to assume Philip was dead, they admitted they had no proof whatsoever. So, Mary continued to hope.

As mothers do, she blamed herself for everything. Before he started his medical degree, she suggested that Philip should see a bit of what a hospital was like. It might put him off or it might fascinate him. It couldn't leave him indifferent. A gap year in London would be good for him, loosen him from her apron strings, open his eyes to the wider world outside Bournemouth. Guy's Hospital was looking for porters and it was half an hour's walk from where his best friend had found a two-room flat in Camberwell. Philip had arranged everything himself in twenty-four hours.

Mary sighed as she thought about it. She should have involved herself in the arrangements. She hadn't properly checked up on Philip's best friend. She hadn't visited the flat. She hadn't taught Philip how to cook. She hadn't talked with him enough about girls. But she had bought him a decent phone contract with unlimited talk-time. And she had put £250 in a bank account for him and found him a good student credit card deal.

He phoned home regularly at first. He said he'd met a lovely student nurse called Elspeth. They had been to a cyclo-cross meet. Her parents lived in Plymouth and both worked for the Royal Navy. She had short auburn hair, freckles and a great sense of fun. The police later said she lived in the nurses' residence close to the hospital. Philip said it was love at first sight. Phone calls became much less frequent. Mary was happy for them both. But Philip rang one February night – just after Valentine's Day – in tears. They had broken up. He said it was Elspeth's fault. He thought she'd found someone else. He never cried normally, not even when his dad died. But now he was clearly heartbroken. He said his flatmate just laughed about it and that made things worse.

He had to find work elsewhere. Elspeth said she didn't want to see Philip ever again. So he'd just started in a new job as receptionist and filing clerk in the palliative care ward, which was in a separate building. There was a backlog of filing for the recently deceased because of the pandemic. Mary tried hard to console him. She suggested he come home for a bit.

That was two years ago. Just thinking about it made her feel guilty. She carried her suitcase upstairs. Philip's bedroom door was open. She walked in. Everything was in place, but there was a distinct depression on his bed like someone had just lain there.

"I'll always believe he's just missing. I know he'll come back," she said aloud.

THE PASSENGER
LOCATOR FORM

Thirty-three-year-old Peter Walker had had a very average, very English life. Secondary school in Romford led to college in Ilford where he managed A-levels in business studies and sport, level three. His dad wanted him to join the army, but Peter was put off by the thought of moving around the whole time. He wanted to stay near London – preferably where he was, in Essex.

Two things dominated his life: football (which meant West Ham) and Nigel Farage. They were linked by beer, the drinking of. He would have supported Farage even if beer didn't come into it. He worshipped him when he was leader of the UK Independence Party; he followed him on Twitter; he liked that Farage was a very good friend of Donald Trump. He had a poster signed by Farage in his bedroom in his parents' house.

He had been abroad only twice, both times to watch West Ham play – once in Spain, once in Germany. He disliked it, abroad that is. The different languages made him feel ill at ease, an outsider. He felt disorientated. He couldn't understand the menus. He didn't like the look of the police, the way they looked at him and his mates. The plain truth was he didn't like foreigners. With all his friends, he voted to leave the EU. The very mention of it made him uncomfortable. He hadn't found a wife. None of the girls he had met wanted to share his interests – drinking, football and Farage.

He fancied the idea of being an entrepreneur in the fitness business, of owning his own company, being his own boss. He realised he would have to cut down on the beer, but he could do that. He had always jogged and kept fit. The growth in the industry had been fantastic in richer parts of the country. Gyms were springing up all over the place, spurred on by the obesity crisis, pressure on women to slim, the influence of role models and sedentary lives spent staring at screens. The suburbs had fewer gyms. There was a niche. But he needed capital to start. So he thought he would take pretty well any job for a couple of years and save hard to pay for his project.

When he got a job as a security guard at Dagenham's engine plant, he found that his employer was actually a massive worldwide service company. It survived on contracts from government to provide staff for one-off jobs at short notice in the health service, for local authorities and for scores of different government bodies. Peter found that once his name and CV was on their books, he was regularly notified of better paid opportunities. He had two brief jobs in local prisons, then as a temporary school caretaker and most recently for Border Control in Tilbury Docks. Out of the blue, he was offered his present job as a contact tracer as part of a large team working to implement the government's drive to reduce covid transmission. They were looking for thorough, tough, no-nonsense telephone operators with common sense. There were incentives based on success rates. The basic pay was excellent. Peter Walker was their man.

Kristina Ivanov was Peter Walker's polar opposite. She was a prima ballerina at the Royal Ballet. She was temperamental, highly intelligent, status-conscious, with the longest legs since Sylvie Guillem. Her technique, her presence, her brilliance on stage was, of course, totally and utterly unknown to Peter Walker. Kristina fled Russia four years earlier, much to the fury of the Kirov Ballet, who had made her what she was. She spoke English with a strong Russian accent. She was a lesbian, yet couldn't admit it in St Petersburg. Now, she was sharing a house in Islington, within walking distance of Sadler's Wells, with her Russian partner, Margarita.

Kristina had just had a terrible forty-eight hours. For the first time in her life, she had been booed. She had been invited to dance as Juliet in Prokofiev's ballet in Paris in a gala celebrating Diaghilev's Ballets Russes. The one rehearsal was disastrous because Romeo told Kristina he had refused to be vaccinated. How could they dance as lovers? Internationally speaking, the timing could not have been worse. The gala was targeted by *Front National* militants and others seeking any occasion to condemn Putin. They almost stopped the performance by demonstrating in the Palais Garnier lobby and then inside the theatre which, by the interval, had been filled with armed police. Not surprisingly, she danced badly. Before she went to bed in the early hours, she tried to fill in the Passenger Locator

Form online. The form drove her mad. It took over an hour because she discovered she didn't have a covid test booking reference number. It didn't help that she was tired, upset and now angry.

Matters were made worse by the journey from Paris on the Eurostar. The sweaty man in the seat next to her in the first class section persistently tried to chat her up. She tried to deter him by working and talking Russian to Margarita on her phone. Then she pretended to fall asleep, but she was uneasy throughout the journey. Back in Islington, Margarita told her that a water main had burst a block away; the house had no water. When it came back on, their hot-water system had an airlock and there was no hot water.

Kristina was still very unhappy with the world when her mobile rang two days later and a rude man from Track and Trace, Peter Walker, announced that a passenger in her Eurostar compartment had tested positive for coronavirus. He had her seat number from the Passenger Locator Form; she had to self-isolate for ten days. She had to stay at her address. The Track and Trace team would call regularly and, if necessary, the police would visit the premises to check she was there. Breaking quarantine was a criminal offence.

A beer-drinking, English chauvinist with no telephone manners was almost bound to clash with a teetotal, female ballet dancer, originally from Russia.

"Who are you to tell me what I can and cannot do?" Kristina shouted into the phone.

"It's the law. It's my job to tell you that if you break the law, you will be prosecuted and, if guilty, fined up to £1,000."

"I am, how do you say, outrageous. You are the drip which makes my bucket flow over. It's no business of yours where I stay. I can stay where I want."

"Actually, legally, no you can't. By law, you have to self-isolate," said the hapless Peter Walker, following his script.

"Look, your Passenger Locator Form is shit. It infringes my human rights. I come to this country from Russia, you understand. Russia. I come because England is free country. I love London. I love England. Now, suddenly you ask with who I travel, what are my travel plans, where I will live, for how long. It's not your business. It's personal information, you understand, personal information. Thanks be to God, we are not in Russia. Completing your locator form is torture. Why you want to know if I have visited any islands when I was in France? What's it got to do with you? And your locator form does not work properly on computer. It is a thing of drunken monkey's dreams."

There was a long silence.

Then Peter Walker said, "Come to think of it, I agree with you. I won't contact you again." And he rang off.

Kristina said, "Bloody bureaucrats." Twice, in Russian.

TANGO

Margaret and Gerald Swan enjoyed life. They were both in their forties and told those who asked that Gerald had sold his company in the renewable energy industry for a fortune. He said he had made a machine that cut crystalline silicon into the millimetre-thin wafers used in solar panels. Most people usually didn't question him further. He said he wanted to spend his retirement on photography and cruising.

He was rarely without his Nikon camera. He loved handling it. It was powerful and sophisticated – qualities he had aspired to during his difficult early life. The camera made him feel in control. At times, it was like a comfort blanket or a pet. (Gerald and Margaret had no children, though they would have loved at least one.) Gerald would seek out other keen photographers and spend hours talking knowledgably about lenses. His hobby made sense given his background in the glass and silicon business. As for cruising, the attractions needed no explanation, at least so it seemed.

There was a side to Gerald that most people, including his

wife, didn't know about, however. It was his relationship to the truth. Gerald's father, who was first a tabloid journalist, then a writer of successful romantic thrillers, disappeared while trying to climb Everest without oxygen when Gerald was six. So, the boy was brought up by his mother alone. Mother and, later, son convinced themselves that no effort had been made to find their brave mountaineer. They bore a grudge against the Foreign Office, the establishment, the insurance company that refused to pay out, even the police as a result.

There was no father at home. Gerald's imagination led him first to exaggerating things, to overdramatising, then to making things up, to fibbing, to distorting the truth. His mother turned a blind eye to it. She thought it was just his way of seeking attention. She would retail his fibs to her friends, beginning with "You wouldn't believe it. Isn't it sweet and he's so young." She joked that Gerald had inherited it from his father, who made up stories for his newspaper to make money.

Unlike his father, Gerald preferred physics, chemistry and maths at school to arts subjects. He won a scholarship to Keble College, Oxford to study engineering science, having impressed at interview with his ideas for harnessing the power of noise, followed by an emotional, somewhat embroidered, account of his father's death on Everest. He found that embellishing the truth made life more interesting. He was in demand for parties. Girls in particular loved the made-up stories about his roommates or experiments in the lab that went disastrously wrong or his method of always winning at bridge. Tweaking the truth was part of his charm. It made people laugh.

Margaret fell for Gerald in Barcelona. She was there to learn Spanish to improve her chances of getting her dream job as an air hostess. He was there to learn about glass-making in Spain. They met at an Irish pub in Las Ramblas. She found him a bit eccentric, a bit wild, mysterious and romantic. They married five years later.

As an air hostess, Margaret chose long-haul flight rotas whenever she could because they usually involved two-day layovers at the destination – Barbados, Trinidad or, best of all, Buenos Aires. She had always loved dancing, but she discovered the tango in Argentina – and that was something in a league of its own. She became bitten by the tango bug and infected Gerald with it, too. They developed near-perfect dance routines. But after ten years of tango, Gerald became stale and wanted to move on. Margaret was still passionate about it, though. The first plangent, menacing notes of the bandoneon or button accordion sent a thrill through her spine like no other. She became entranced, would fuse her body to Gerald's, gripping him like ivy round a tree trunk. In London, there were never enough milongas or tango parties to satisfy her. She became an addict. They thought of buying a villa in Buenos Aires, but Gerald persuaded her that she could dance tango every night on a cruise so they settled for six months of cruising every year.

The problem was Gerald didn't have the money. As was his way, he had completely exaggerated the 'fortune' made from selling his business, but had never come clean with Margaret about it. The paltry proceeds of the sale could not sustain the glamourous lifestyle she had always wanted. Cruising cost £100,000 for six months for the two of them.

Margaret had no savings of her own. Gerald quickly started accumulating debts. He loved her and didn't want her to have to worry.

So, he had to find a way of funding his cost-of-living crisis. His background in the glass industry proved to be a godsend. Their first cruise took them to Trinidad. In a rum shop by the Savannah in Port of Spain, Gerald met a jeweller who specialised in emeralds. Back at his house, after several rum and cokes, Gerald was shown an exquisite emerald necklace with a gold clasp. The jeweller said it was worth $150,000, that he had bought it in Guyana, and that, of course, it was genuine. The jeweller produced a certificate from the Swiss Gemmological Institute. Gerald could have it for a special price of $135,000. The jeweller knew that Gerald's cruise ship was leaving at 7pm and it was already teatime. He thought he could make a quick sale.

But the jeweller was unlucky. He had met his match as a high risk-taker. Gerald could tell that the emeralds were synthetic. They had been created in a laboratory. They sparkled too fiercely and had no flaws. He confronted the jeweller saying that he was a fraudster; the emeralds were fake; the certificate was fake; he would call the police; he would close down his business. Unless, unless they did a deal. He would buy the necklace for $1,000 cash, provided the jeweller gave him a receipt for $150,000. And so it was.

Gerald presented the necklace to Margaret at the dinner table the same evening as the cruise ship left Trinidad. He took pictures of the occasion and took a close-up picture of the necklace itself for the insurance company, the same company that had refused to pay out on his father's death.

The fake emerald necklace he bought for $1,000 he insured as a genuine one for $150,000, backed up by the Swiss certificate, the fake receipt and photographs. Gerald waited patiently for a month for the insurance policy itself.

Gerald then had to organise the 'theft'. On the next cruise, Margaret wore the necklace every night at dinner for a week and in particular while dancing a demonstration tango with him. In that way, hundreds of passengers and crew saw it. Margaret did not wear it on the last evening of the cruise, however, when virtually all cabins were empty as passengers partied the night away. She had spent some time beforehand hiding the necklace in her hand luggage. As the huge cruise ship (5000 passengers and 2000 crew) anchored at the Port of Miami, the cruise capital of the world, Gerald and Margaret reported that their cabin had been burgled and the necklace stolen. Passengers were already disembarking. The ship's purser could only suggest they report it to the police and their insurance company, which they did.

It was six months after that, while they were on another Caribbean cruise, that the insurance company paid up. Margaret and Gerald are still cruising somewhere. The only way you might recognise them is when they dance the tango brilliantly. Oh, and from the way they both cheat at bridge.

THE LAST LAUGH

Often on Saturday mornings, Henry and I would have a man-chat on the phone. It all started when we learnt at about the same time that we had stage four cancer and needed cheering up. Our calls were morale boosting and not meant to last more than ten minutes. We'd start by checking each other's secondary health problems – my kidney stones that kept recurring and Henry's back, which he was convinced was a slipped disc. Then we'd tell each other anything really important about our families, like whether we'd seen our children or whether they were still thinking of emigrating and, if so, would it be Auvergne or Brittany. Then we'd say libellous things about the government or about one of our sportsmen for losing at rugby, tennis or cricket, especially cricket. Finally, we'd boast about our latest DIY exploits, which were rarely finished or properly done. There was a running joke about my unsuccessful attempts to fix the light in our shower.

"Ollie, are you still showering in the dark?" he would say.

"Sometimes," I'd reply. "I thought it was the switch, but since I changed it, the light over the basin has also gone out."

He would laugh. So I would tease him about his inability to start his strimmer.

"I haven't had time to dismantle it. Anyway, I've decided to have a wilderness. What's good enough for the Prince of Wales is good enough for me."

Both our prognoses were for about five years. Mine was slightly longer than Henry's. Sometimes our chats took a fatalistic turn, sometimes a defiant one. Today, it was the second.

"Oliver, we've decided, or rather I've decided, to move," Henry announced at the beginning of our chat.

I almost spluttered into my coffee. "What do you mean?" I asked.

"We're moving back to London. I'm fed up with this house. It's too old and cold. And the couple opposite are evil."

"Henry, what's come over you? I'm shocked. We've lived in this part of Kent – what, three miles from each other – for the best part of twenty years."

"Exactly. It's nothing personal, but it's probably too long in one place."

"But you've invested half your life in your house and garden. The house used to be a ruin. You've restored it beautifully – the beams, the magnificent fireplace, those lovely leaded-light windows, your studio in the old stables."

"Quite. It's done, finished. I want to turn the page."

"This is so sudden, Henry. What's it all about?"

There was a pause. "With the time that I've got left, I

want something more, some fun. And the couple opposite have driven me mad. It started with her – Marigold – who now claims to be Maria Callas reincarnate. She sings opera day and night, accompanying her stereo in her sitting room. It's twenty yards from our front room, for God's sake. The racket is appalling. She murders everything she sings from Verdi to Wagner. She can't sing. I think she might be deaf."

"Have you asked her to stop? Or at least to sing in tune."

"Of course. But each time I've approached her, it's actually got worse. She says there's no law against singing in one's own home."

"What about asking her husband to do something?"

Henry laughed. "Quentin? Impossible. He's as mad as a March hare himself. He thinks he's Master of the South Weald Hunt. He's dressed in hunting clothes every day: cutaway coat, breeches, riding hat. He sits on his exercise bicycle, what, ten yards from our front gate, straight after breakfast, whipping the machine and blowing his blasted hunting horn. He's barking mad."

I should have said that Henry and his wife, Frances, live in one of the prettiest villages in Kent, almost as attractive as mine. Their house is in a tiny lane off the village green, which has the usual features – pub, manor house, duck pond, post box, shop. Eccentrics are not unknown in the village. The previous vicar came from Cumbria and was a mountaineer ("I'm closer to God at the top of Ben Nevis," he would say). He was frustrated in Kent where there were no mountains. But he had to test himself, so he took up marathon running. Most of the races were on Sundays when he should have been taking his church services. The archbishop told him to retire early.

On the phone a week later, Henry seemed even more troubled. I thought he might have had another argument with Marigold or Quentin. But no. He said he wanted to share a moral dilemma with me.

"The estate agent from Canterbury has been round while Frances was at the hairdressers," he said. "You'll never believe what he said our asking price should be. Three million! He said clients would be lining up to buy it. Buyers wanted peace and quiet, tranquillity and a big garden."

"Wonderful. But I'm still sorry that you're leaving. Where will you go to?"

"Chelsea. Where the action is." (He'd left London twenty-five years ago and was out of touch.)

"To paint the town red while I still can. But my problem is that I didn't tell the agent about the neighbours. By a miracle, they were not performing when he was here. Perhaps I should ring the agent and tell him."

"Absolutely not," I said. "You aren't responsible for your neighbours. *Caveat emptor* is the expression, isn't it? It's the buyer's problem. Forget it. You're quite right to have a last fling in Chelsea. Go for it, Henry."

The following Saturday when I rang, it was Frances who answered. She said Henry was still asleep. He'd not been feeling too well the past week. His liver had been playing up; the doctor had been round and prescribed stronger painkillers and sleeping pills. It was awkward because the agent couldn't bring clients to see the house while Henry was in bed. Foolishly, I didn't pursue things. I thought it best not to bother them too much.

When I rang a week later, Frances said she was about to ring me with awful news. The evening before, Henry was running a big fever and became delirious. He said his heart felt funny. She dialled 999. While she was phoning, Henry had got out of bed, moved the stereo speakers to the front window, which he'd opened, and was playing Bizet's *Carmen* at full volume.

"When I got to the window myself," she said, quite calmly, "to see what on earth was going on, I saw Marigold and Quentin by their front door with their hands over their ears. Henry, in his pyjamas, was laughing like a maniac. His face was quite white and he was sweating. 'Serves you bloody right. Now you know what it's like,' he shouted. Those were his last words. Before I could reach him, he'd collapsed in a heap on the carpet. The ambulance arrived about an hour too late. He died a happy man. He felt he'd had the last laugh."

THE CABIN

It had happened before. Once. When Susanne went to England to buy a dog and Robin was alone for ten days. But that was in the spring. Now it was September and Susanne was off to a painting workshop in Nova Scotia. When they said goodbye at the airport in Montreal, Robin said he would take the opportunity to replace the fly-screens at the cabin and maybe cut some of the undergrowth, which was creeping closer to the old building every year. Like the last time, he had an overwhelming wish to cast himself adrift on the lake, to cut himself off from all the pressures of work, other people, events, even family. The last time, it had ended badly: he was caught in a spring thunderstorm, lightning struck the water around him and the canoe filled with rainwater in five minutes.

The cabin, the lake and the forest around it, deep in Quebec's Laurentians, were as much a part of Robin's life as his smile or his quirky dress sense. His signature wardrobe was leather waistcoats and coloured socks. He'd spent half his summers in that wild corner of Canada as a boy fifty years ago while his father wrote his books, fished and built the boathouse. It was a two-hour drive north from Montreal and he reached the place as dusk was falling. There was time to lay a fire, heat up a chicken pie from the overflowing bag of groceries (he always brought too much food) and watch the sky change colour with a whisky in his hand.

Alarm clocks were unnecessary at the cabin. The dawn chorus was almost deafening after the city. Robin filled a thermos with coffee, then put bread, sliced sausage and an apple into a canvas shoulder bag. There was no need to lock the cabin door. The building was a mile from the road, down an unmarked track. It had never been burgled.

The boathouse was hidden from the cabin by knee-high grass, which obscured the path as Robin strode down to the lakeside. It was shortly after 5am and the sun was peeping over the pines. At the boathouse, he had to stop for a full minute to look at the mist lying on the lake like a blanket of cotton wool. August had been hot and the water was still relatively warm, certainly warm enough for a swim. It was a tempting thought. He swam all year round. Swimming in his own lake, with no one watching but the ducks, was unspeakably pleasurable. He walked to the end of the wooden jetty and inhaled deeply. Dawn had a special earthy smell.

The movements for opening the boathouse, turning his canoe the right way up and carrying it to the jetty with the paddle were second nature. So, too, was the way he settled into it and pushed off silently. Silence was important, both for him internally and his relationship with the natural world. He dipped his paddle noiselessly, expertly, into the dark water. The sound of the drips of water at the beginning and end of each thrusting stroke accompanied the rippling of the wavelets and disturbed nothing.

Man and canoe effortlessly followed the reedy shoreline for five minutes. After twenty strokes, with the canoe's nose pointed towards where the lake curved, Robin stopped paddling, laid the paddle in the canoe and sat still. The sun slowly rose to make the water change colour from grey to green. The wavelets flashed and splashed gently, a myriad of mirrors as far as the eye could see. Quacking mallards were looking for breakfast at the edge of the rush bank. Two loons overtook them, low in the water, swimming fast, heads erect. Then one dived and disappeared for ten seconds. Loon, coot and grebe were not flattering names by comparison with other ducks he knew – goldeneye, redhead, harlequin. But each had a place in the lake.

Paddling back towards the reeds and sedge, he heard a twig-snapping noise and gasped in awe at the sight of a moose with majestic antlers. It had its front legs apart as it dropped its head to drink at the water's edge, quite unconcerned by Robin's canoe. Immediately behind it was a belt of black and dark-green spruce and pines. Not far to left and right were maples, ash and birch. The maple leaves had started to change colour to yellow ochre and red. Nature was about to put on its spectacular seasonal show. The sun had burned through the mist and was lighting the woods with a blaze of colour.

In a semi-trance, Robin thought of how privileged he was to be here. There was something spiritual as well as something primeval about the water, the wildfowl and the woods. It made him alive in a way it was difficult to articulate, like listening to Beethoven or Chopin. The lake had changed him over a lifetime from being just a watcher of the wonders of nature to a participant. And there was something soothing about lakes. You couldn't be stressed on a lake like this.

It was a time in his life to reflect on where he'd gone wrong; where he'd made a difference; what he'd wished he'd done sooner; why he was both happy and sad. It was a time to draw conclusions.

He wished he'd realised much sooner that his mother's regular illnesses were also appeals for help and that he had recognised sooner her signs of depression. He wished he'd been more attentive to his sister and brother, and less obsessed with his own career. He wished he'd spent more time with his parents before it was too late.

On the trivial side – and he smiled as he thought about it – he wished he'd taken courses on electricity, cookery, combustion engines and dog management.

What made him happy was how magnificent his children – *their* children – were and how amazing the eight grandchildren were. Susanne was a glorious mother and a sublime wife. That made him ridiculously happy.

He thought of something Pope Francis had just said: being happy wasn't about having a perfect life. Sometimes we have to use pain to tune in to pleasure. Never give up on being happy, he said, because life is an incredible spectacle.

A lake trout arching upwards beside the canoe to catch an unwary fly brought his thoughts back to the blissful natural world around him.

And this, ironically, is what made him sad. This wonderful world was under such threat – more than that. It was disappearing faster and faster, year by year, like a runaway train. All because of our ignorance, thoughtlessness, selfishness and irresponsibility. There were fewer ducks, moose, fish, even pine woods than when he was a boy. But for years, he hadn't taken enough notice or really wondered why.

He picked up his paddle, turned the canoe round with a dozen strokes and headed back to the wooden jetty. His paddling was furious. The canoe leapt forwards with each strike. The water ran down his arms, wetting his trousers and shirt. He reached the grey boards of the old jetty in five minutes. A rope tied the boat to a post in an instant.

He wanted somehow to embrace this disappearing world one last time, to hug it, to thank it for all it meant to him. He took off his shoes first, then all his other clothes, left them on the jetty and jumped into the lake.

Matador

For exclusive discounts on Matador titles,
sign up to our occasional newsletter at
troubador.co.uk/bookshop